LEA^{THE}VINGS

SUE L CLARKE

**Grosvenor House
Publishing Limited**

This book is published by
Grosvenor House Publishing Ltd
28-30 High Street, Guildford, Surrey, GU1 3EL.
www.grosvenorhousepublishing.co.uk

A CIP record for this book
is available from the British Library

ISBN 978-1-78148-716-7

For my wonderful family.

ACKNOWLEDGEMENTS

Thank you to my fantastic parents and family, without whom I wouldn't have made it this far.

A very special thank you to my wonderful daughters who have given me every reason to succeed and to Frosty for supporting me throughout.

I am enormously grateful to the friends who have loyally stood by me through thick and thin; you know who you are. A very special mention for my two best friends, Gill and Julie, who have stood by me on the darkest of days.

To Hannah Shillito, my warmest thanks for producing the most wonderful photograph for my front cover.

And finally, a big thank you to the poor devils who I work with - who have answered my endless questions and always been behind me.

It has taken me ten years to complete my book and with the help of Grosvenor House Publishing Company, I have realised the dream I first had, when I was seven years old.

Follow me at: 'suelclarke.com'.

Rolls Royce
Wishing on a Star

I think I might be dead, but not dead dead. Maybe this is the result of having one Bacardi too many last night. Somehow this felt very different and I wasn't quite sure what was going on. I closed my eyes to try and get my bearings.

OK so life hadn't turned out quite as I'd expected, but I'm beginning to suspect that it doesn't for anyone. It is possible that some people are much better at concealing it than others or have better skin or handsome bone structure that doesn't show the damage of trauma or the ravages of life. There are of course those who have ridiculously happy faces who can't even look sad if they want to. I refer of course to the Anneka Rice and Richard Bransons of this world and more recently Martin Clunes' plummy, chummy grin and the head nodding chirpiness of Michael McIntyre. Ugh. That damned shininess just makes me yearn for the honest furrowed brow of Rigsby in *Rising Damp* and the unbotoxed, yet real face of Dame Judi Dench.

The strains of *Wishing on a Star* faded, to be replaced by *I'm not in love* by 10cc. Now I know that something is wrong as this song was banned in my collection along with Sad Café and most of the Bee Gees' songs.

This was bad, very bad I could feel those memories swirling in a musical fog and taking me back to places I'd really rather not go. It was a familiar pain like tooth ache or labour pains. Something was seriously wrong and the world was going darker; a strange crackling sound began to make my head fizz, then an electric flash of bright light.....

I began to come round. Wow, if this was a migraine it was a very musical one! My head was throbbing in time with the base in *Final Countdown* and some vague distant muttering. Oh God, I *am* dead!! Maybe I've had one of those brain things that kill you on the spot? I needed to pull myself together or I'd be the one flying over the cuckoo's nest. Very slowly I managed to open my eyes and I realised that I was no longer in my own bed, or my own bedroom for that matter.

I found myself lying on a bed that was very similar to a hospital bed. I was wearing a white plastic suit and a visor and straight in front of me was a TV screen. Oh God. Aliens!!! I comforted myself with the thought that if they had felt the urge to do an anal probe I must have missed it. Unless that's why they had woken me!! Christ on a bike what the hell was going on!!!!! I took some deep breaths, gritted my teeth and said a quick prayer to my childhood heroes from *Little House on the Prairie*. The problem had always been that I would probably have been cast as Half Pint rather than the very pretty blind Mary. I needed to stop rambling and get a grip or wake up. Strangely I knew deep down that this was my new reality. What I'd do for a cigarette right now would put anyone to shame. OK, time to look around and take in my surroundings in my *Space Odyssey* new home. Yep, as I thought I couldn't move, my suit appeared to be attached to some sort of main frame by a thick white umbilicus. Oh hell! Am I feeding from the mother planet, is it sucking out my substance to go into the greater good?? I had to calm myself, terror was taking over and in the distance I could hear voices. Suddenly a voice boomed into my helmet and I jumped out of my plastic skin. It gave automated instructions like the safety drill on an aeroplane.

'Don't pull the cord!'

'Don't ever lift the visor under any circumstances.'

'Don't move suddenly.'

'The emergency hatch is to your left, marked with a red cross and to the left .....' The droning voice was fading as dizziness embraced me, sleep was imminent, far too much information. Then a pink light filled the room and I closed my eyes.

'Let's put her on snooze' said a male voice which was disturbingly familiar.

'*I said* we should put her on snooze.' insisted a female voice, in a much firmer tone.

It was her, her voice, I knew it and tried to place it and resigned myself to the 'weirdest nightmare of all time' theory. Perhaps I had mistakenly bought a bottle of Russian Bacardi like that Vodka that was really cleaning fluid. This was unlikely as I shop at Asda. I began to feel a cowardly whimper coming on.

'Good lord - going soft are we?' unmistakably an Alan Rickman sneer.

This Russian Bacardi had some strange powers, I thought to myself, it could be the new heroin.

'Your timing is off, as usual. She's confused Alan, this could be an overload!'

She then addressed me directly it sounded just like … well like Dame Judi Dench!! One of my favourite actresses of all time.

'We can only give you six clicks I'm afraid Helena. Try not to worry, it's all very confusing at first. Rickman would you press the release at once, press the release or I *will* report you!!' she demanded.

'Too soft woman, there's work to be done… and call me Flint everyone else does.'

I hear the clicks, then blackout.

Calling occupants of interplanetary craft
Carpenters

'For goodness sake Flint, switch that music off, we need her to concentrate.' I opened my eyes to the white sterile room and the flickering screen.

'You forget yourself, she'll hear you. Could I do the introductions? I'm sure you have more pressing things to do and I can give Helena a somewhat gentler introduction.'

'Always the same! I get the dried out alcoholic dowsed in his own self pity. His theme, remorse. How unique!! He'll be banging on about being anally retentive with lashings of childhood deprivation. Bollocks!'

'She's awake. Go to 7 at once, after all you have other clients who need you.'

A click in my left ear, a crackle of static and I'm back with Dame Judi Dench nick name 'Pink'. 'What a blinder of an evening to return to the same dream.'

'It's not.' she stated quite plainly.

'Not what?' I asked.

'A dream.' she said wearily.

A pause. Oh my God she can hear what I'm thinking.

'Yes she can.' she retorted. 'And to be quite frank it's quite a mess in there, which is why you're here. I will, of course explain.'

The lights flickered and there was a short blast of a siren.

'Two hours until 'Plenni', that means replenishments and is a chance for you to meet some of our other clients. Ample time if we're not interrupted. I could of course implant the information straight into your cortex. Flint would without question.'

'Is Flint, um is he Alan Rickman - the actor... from *Die Hard*?' I ask confused.

'Alan Rickman, why yes of course, didn't you recognise his voice?'

'Well yes, but how did you both get into my head?'

'I was just saying that I would like to explain, Flint would have just implanted without question, but it's so impersonal and there's always something lacking.' Pink paused. 'Anyway, pay attention and remove the frown, it won't help.'

I began to feel panicky. Why hadn't the alarm clock gone off? Why hadn't I struggled to the toilet and flicked on the kettle? This was going on for way too long and it was too detailed to be one of my usual jigsaw nightmares.

'I am trying to help you. Would you at least try to listen to me! Or shall I call Flint, he may bring the probe. Your choice, of course.'

'No, no.... I'm good, honestly.'

'Just my little joke about the probe as you brought it up.' Pink chuckled to herself.

'Great! Thanks er... Pink. Hilarious. Just what I needed.'

There was a pause. I decided to close my eyes and concentrate, desperately trying to empty my mind, but couldn't help think of *Children of the damned*.

'Helena! I really cannot see the point if you're just going to go off at a tangent and waste my time. No wonder you have issues, and it's *Village of the Damned*!! not *Children of the damned*. Good lord!' she paused and then quietly said, 'Well I suppose it was made in 1960. There now we really must move on.' I lay back, a captive audience beginning to feel trapped in a surrealistic version of *Space Odyssey*!

'Helena!' Pink took a deep breath.

'It's quite straightforward really.' Another pause. 'You see you came to us last Friday to be exact. It was quite a challenge getting you through. Bit of a mix up in quality. Anyway...'

'Do you mean I've died!!! Is that is?'

'Told her she's dead yet?' interrupted Flint. I could almost see the sardonic smile on his face.

I'm dead, I'm dead.!!! Am I really dead? Perhaps I'm on a life support machine and my brain's just beginning to wake up. Like in E.R. once before George Clooney was famous, when he was just a good looking young actor.'

'Helena. Please try and concentrate. I'm afraid that you're in, well, you're in a transitional state, not dead actually.' She paused and my train of thought tailed off, as the pit of my stomach contracted.

'It's complicated. You're just at a kind of cross roads, that's the best way I can explain it. Don't panic, Flint and I are your Guides and here to help you. To be perfectly honest I think you'll find that I'll be the most help, but you did select us both. Now we really must move on.'

'So I'm not dead then or drugged or pissed?'

'No, none of those, you are however running late and I need to explain more about what will happen.'

'If you look down to your right you will see the fluorescent pink balls glowing in their Perspex squares. Do you see them?' she asked.

I nodded. It felt invasive, she knew exactly what I was thinking. I didn't like it at all. Not one bit.

'We're not really interested in your likes and dislikes Helena.' snarled Flint.

'Kindly return to 3 at once!' a new voice boomed from behind me. It was the voice of Anthony Hopkins and demanded obedience. Perhaps I was trapped on a rather bad film set or ... 'How rude!' interrupted Pink. 'If you don't mind it was you who selected us!! Not Hopkins of course, he's the compulsory collective.'

Pink was offended. Dream or no dream I had made a serious blunder. They were probably greasing up the probe right now.

'So, I picked you, Dame Judi, as my guide and matched you up with Alan Rickman and he calls you Pink and you call him Flint. Apart from that it's just a normal day!'

'That's correct, and you may like to know that there are others here – that's where Flint is now, seeing one of his other cases.'

'Sorry.' I muttered to myself. 'I've never been dead before and....'

'I'll continue.' said Pink. I sensed forgiveness. 'There are 8 pink balls all glowing. They represent unresolved issues, events, maybe even moments in your life. It's quite simple my dear everyone has their own theme and you do know about these issues already.' said Pink.

'It's leaving.' said Flint quite bluntly. 'Your theme, it's leaving, people, places, times you know. Strong theme, should be, well, interesting.'

'Enough! 6 clicks, at once. She's drifting.!!' insisted Pink.

My head pounded, my heart was banging away.
I felt sick again.
The static crackled and the screen went dead.

The theme from *Mash* floated through my head. Ah I must have fallen asleep on the settee watching TV. Oh and by the way I'm 13. Maybe it's a Wednesday night and mum and dad are just upstairs getting ready to go out. I'm losing it aren't I? Maybe I'm going insane...

'Don't flatter yourself! That's just your normal state of mind.' stated Flint.

Suddenly a fluorescent light switched on and I was cruelly thrust back or forward into my white shiny world, still in my plastic suit. Disappointment flowed through me like cold soup. What now, what next? I could hear a wicked chuckle it was Flint's voice, but in the distance.

'It's not even remotely amusing!' clipped Pink. A rising chorus of '*Suicide is painless.*' became louder and louder.

'I put it on for Number 7.' said Flint.

'That's fairly obvious and so inappropriate, now switch it off before the Panel hear it! Besides it's just not that funny Flint.'

Pink's tone changed, became more assertive as she addressed me.

'Helena, good morning. May I apologise for Flint.' A pause, no reply was necessary, it was more of a statement.

'Now then,' she said in a conciliatory tone. 'You do remember our discussion, more importantly do you remember your theme?'

'Yes leaving. I was intending to ask...'

'Well don't, there's no time.'

Flint blurted in, 'I'm afraid that I must depart to listen to the pretentious babble from Number 7. Such are the burdens of popularity!'

'Who..?' I began.

'Who is the top guide? Richard Burton – he's number one again this month, much overrated I'd say. Why don't you ask Pink about her rating?' Flint's voice chuckled in anticipation.

'I hardly think that *Die Hard and Truly Madly Deeply* put you in the same category as Mr. Burton or royalty!' sniped Pink.

'Did you hear that harsh tone Helena? Pink is merely referring to the popularity of Gary Barlow and Kate Middleton. Ha!' he scoffed and chuckled to himself and then clicked himself off.

'Is it true people pick Kate?' I asked. 'Do they get her?'

'Not always, no. It is true that David Beckham and Oprah Winfrey are both very popular.' Pink paused. 'I select my clients of course, it's in the agreement.' Pink coughed, seemingly embarrassed.

'Are you really Dame Judi and is the other voice Alan Rickman – really? and can you really read my thoughts?' I was beginning to panic now.

'The answer is yes to all those things and there is no need to keep repeating yourself.'

'Why does he call you Pink?'

'It's just a nickname.'

'Where does it come from and...'

'Rickman's is Flint, his nickname.'

'Would you stop reading my mind!' Helena yelled furiously.

'Yes, I can see that must be irritating, we're under such pressure you see, the way the hours are allocated. I can imagine this is very hard for you...'

'Do I get to hear this definition?'

'Um. Why yes of course - A very hard, fine-grained quartz that sparks when struck with steel. So you can see what I mean?'

I can hear the sound of Flint laughing in the distance.

'Am I really dead Pink?' I asked, my mind a blur.

'Not dead so much as dormant, you'll see.' she paused. 'It's really rather a shock I know – you are quite young anyway let's move on, perhaps in time after the process...' she stopped abruptly.

'Perhaps what?' I asked desperately, maybe there was some sort of reprieve.

'Helena, I'm simply not permitted to say anymore. My purpose is clear cut and we must...' Pink was rudely interrupted by the strains of *Little ole wine drinker me* drifting over the headphones. It stopped abruptly and I'm sure I could faintly hear the muttering of Flint in the background.

'Enough.' insisted Pink. 'Now the new ball is glowing as you can see and it's ready for loading. The remote in front of you is similar to that of a TV and easy to operate, you will be in full control.'

'Will I be there? I mean actually there, in my own past?' I asked

'Yes, as an observer, unseen but watching and learning. It may be that you have merely misunderstood events or misremembered. It's common in childhood selections.'

'Have you shown her yet?' blurted Flint. 'Good God these are the easy ones woman. I'm in the midst of number 7 self harming with a ruler in his pre-pubescent period, whatever that means!'

'Kindly leave this to me Flint. This may be a joint case, but I'm clearly superior at the introductory infusion.' There was no mistaking Pink's tone.

Pink sighed and then a slight pause.

'You may ask one more question before loading, time is precious.'

'Do you know what it is, this memory or incident or whatever it is?' I was getting nervous.

'Yes.' Pink said kindly. 'There's nothing to fear. Just relax and...'

There was a clicking of static and streams of pink light. I seemed to be propelled through the screen into a white antiseptic room. In front of me a child sat on her mother's knee and a doctor with a silver mirror on his head was speaking and peering into the child's ears. My ears, as I am that child.

'You can move around Helena.' advised Pink.

I knew this scene, I remembered it vividly. I'm 5 years old. I smile at seeing my mum looking so young, concern etched on her face as she supports both me and teddy. But there's something wrong with the scene. The doctor is explaining something very carefully and my mother nods, a frown creasing her forehead. I look at myself, all tense and rigid, clinging tightly to my teddy and I know I'm thinking about my 'I Spy book of hospitals' and wondering if I will be able to tick all the boxes and get my badge. The excitement of the white lights and the harsh antiseptic smell and the seriousness of the doctors with circular mirrors strapped to their heads for some ungodly reason, had worn off. Then I realise I'm not looking up, but counting the white daisies on my floral frock. I begin to pull at teddy's paw patched with some flannelette sheeting that mum had sewn on to stop the sawdust from seeping out. It's not because I'm rude or even bored. I suddenly realise it's because I can't hear.

'You were going deaf; this is an emergency admittance to a hospital out of the local area.'

I looked at myself, hair in bunches, white socks, T bar sandals as I skip innocently down a shiny white corridor, still secure.

The screen flickers and I'm sat on the bed with teddy as my mother hugs me and mouths some silent words. As a child I'm innocently unconcerned as this is just the beginning of my big adventure. My head is crammed full of Enid Blyton's adventurous children and my *I spy* book as my mum leaves the ward. I get changed, bathed and weighed by Nurse Linda. I rationalise the situation thinking that things must be OK as Linda is also my middle name. Then I see my chance and I'm off down endless corridors searching for clues that I can tick off in my book. My face is set determined as I embark on my excellent adventure. But they find me, I'm staring up at a huge bed and watching a big machine pump up and down. I couldn't work out what I'd found, the machine would have had to have a long name. They put me in bed and then a strange nurse approaches me with a 'real' needle, which was definitely not part of the game.

I wake up and nurse Linda spoons ice cream down my burning throat. I look down on my pale face and recognise the shock that my books had not prepared me for – the reality.

'You're starting to realise.' cuts in Pink. 'Now look at your face.'

The screen flickers.

I'm stood in the ward facing my 5 year old self. I'm wearing a tangerine nylon nightie, not allowed these days because of the fire risk. I keep looking at the door, I'm waiting for something. I'm swinging my legs against the side of my bed, even teddy has been discarded. My face is set and my mouth is flat lining, eyes bruised with misunderstanding, brain ticking, trying to remember.

No one came. The boy in the next bed sat upright as his parents bustled in with boy's comics and bottles of squash. His mother spoke to me, I looked at her again through my 40 year old eyes, she was genuine, but not to me at 5.

'Would you like some comics?' she asked me kindly.

I rudely turned my back as my eyes stung with nettle tears. Nurse Linda rescued me and swung me round and round for a long time. I went into the adjoining old people's ward and rode the huge rough rocking horse, wearing no knickers.

The scene flickered. I'm sat back on the bed again in my coat and shoes. I'm going somewhere, but terrified no one will come. Perhaps they'll leave me here, I thought and Nurse Linda will take me home and swing me round in her front room until I grow too heavy.

'Look at your face!' instructs Pink.

My mother anxiously enters the ward, she looks tired and upset. I won't look at her; I purse my 5 year old lips and look away. I remembered not speaking to her as she hugged me and gently put a lamb's wool beret over my head, pulling it down gently over my ears. The ears that could now listen to what it was too late to hear. I looked at my brown currant eyes set like stones in a white face and a veil of insecurity flickered across them.

'Can you see it Helena?' she asked. 'The shift.'

'Yes I do. I see it now.'

Of course the explanation was less dramatic and my poor mother suffered more than I did. I had been rushed into a hospital 30 miles away from home. My father was working away and my mother could not drive and had my sister to look after. Quite straightforward and no-one's fault. I was off school for some time and ate mountains of ice cream.

Then the worst shock of all, mum and dad took me back!! Back to the hell hole ! I was sat in a waiting room, considering my fate and watching a light that changes from red to green. Perhaps if I'm green, I can go home. No such luck, it seemed to turn green for everyone in the end. I'm led into a room, the smell, the white and the dreaded needle too much to cope with. I faint. I'm anaemic. My new found insecurity ricocheting around my head, the memory and association now firmly stamped into my emotional make up.

The screen flickered. I was returned to my pod. I glanced down at the other balls in trepidation. Weariness now pumped through my veins.

'Close her down Flint, she's had enough!' shouted Pink.

'Why that was child's play.' he responded. The world went black and a menthol smell filled my head, like strong felt pens, a blessed relief.

'*Leaving on a jet plane*
Don't know when I'll be back again.'
John Denver

I smiled to myself as I struggled to wake up. On hearing the song I quickly realised that I was now the target of Flint's humour. Pink shut it down, of course.

'Good morning Helena. As you missed Plenni yesterday, we had to auto infuse you. We think that it may be a good idea for you to meet your neighbours. I'm sure that it will help you to, well to adapt.' stated Pink in a business like fashion.

'I have already warned you about number 7, waster.' chipped in Flint. Pink ignored him.

'Now you'll just meet three of our client base today,' she paused. 'Sadly we lost number 8 last night. A tragic case. Don't ask me to explain....'

'You don't need to.' Flint interrupted. 'He selected Jeremy Kyle and Ruby Wax as his guides! A kind of insincere American chat show hell!'

I heard Pink giggle, the wicked giggle for which she is famous. She coughed and then composed herself.

'Today in Plenni, you will meet number 3 – theme addiction, number 5 theme ambition and number 7 who is as you know, due to Flint's indiscretion, is an alcoholic. No last names here. Oh and you're 2 by the way. We simply plug you into the connective circlet and that's it. We will **not** interrupt you or listen...'

'That's not strictly true. There was one occasion when number 22 overdosed on silver and attempted to unplug the main loop!' Flint said mischievously.

'Flint! Desist!' snapped Pink. 'Now then Helena, I'll just flick this switch and you will be transported to the circlet. It's terribly complex and... .'

Pink paused. 'No Helena, you won't be meeting Jean Luc Pickard, it's not that glamorous. This isn't *Star Trek*!' she added.

'Press the switch, for God's sake woman!' shouted Flint. 'They're waiting!'

A switch well and truly clicked. I opened my eyes in a room with dimmed lighting and a superimposed backdrop of a blue sky punctuated with multi coloured whirling planets. I wriggle in my seat and shake my head to bring myself round. I'm sat upright at a white table and there is no white suit. I've got my body back!! I look down at my legs clad in blue jeans and pat them. They feel real. I move my head from side to side and enjoy freedom from the restrictive helmet. I notice that I'm wearing a white standard T shirt. The lighting is subdued and as I become comfortable in my clothes. Strains of 80's music waft through the air, making everything seem even more surreal. I shake my head again and refocus. Facing me is a young woman in her mid twenties, she's dressed in the same jeans and T shirt. She has bubbly black hair and piercing blue eyes which flicker with mischief.

'First time?' she asks flashing me a friendly smile.

'How come we don't have our suits on?' I feel like, well like I'm alive!! Am I the only one that's dead or are you all dead?'

'I'm afraid we collectively think that we are all bleedin' dead.' But none of us have a fuckin' clue. All we know is this is **our** time, this time in Plenni before they split us all up again and we don't get long. Look, meet the gang and then we'll talk, but carefully, OK?'

'Yep.' I gulp and bite my nails nervously. I'm aware that there are two other people sat either side of me.

'Well I'm 3.' she adds directly. 'The name's Shauna, addictive personality, alcohol, drugs - you name it I've loved it!'

I nod and smile cautiously, then carefully attempt to remove a half bitten nail from the corner of my mouth.

'Bad habit that!' wines a deep Welsh voice coming from my left. It belongs to a slim, attractive man in his late twenties. A mop of strawberry blond hair crowns a handsome face, his perfect teeth giving a winning smile. He is also dressed in the same jeans and t-shirt.

'I'm 5. Andy.' I nod in recognition. 'Over ambitious, salesman slash entrepreneur. No morals isn't it?' He shrugs his shoulders, but before he can elaborate we are interrupted.

'I'm 7, the name's Barry.' states a middle aged man to my right. 'You will of course have heard about me.' he adds smugly in a flat, but well heeled accent. I realise that this is the number 7 that Rickman is always banging on about.

'I am an alcoholic, such a crude term.' His sunken brown eyes lazily attempt to make contact and attempt to crinkle in an unconvincing smile which stretches his sallow skin. Intermittent strands of black hair, like whip strokes, are flicked across a balding head. He seems self absorbed. His face stamped with the evidence of a hard life, an unhealthy one at that.

I begin to gain more confidence, but feel quite apprehensive, as though something is going to happen.

'She's waitin.' states Shauna quite bluntly.

'Pardon. You should really learn to extend your vocabulary, my dear Shauna and I simply must ask why your name is such a hybrid of other names. It's such a shame when people just can't make their minds up and bastardise perfectly suitable....'

'Shut yer face fat boy! I'll give you bastardising, we can vote to have you transferred to a different slot. What about it Taff?'

'Leave it out Shauna, we're none of us perfect. Now then what was it you meant with the waiting?' asks Andy. I look over to Shauna and raise my shoulders in a shrug.

'Don't worry kid, the voices are off- no intrusion, no interruptin' the guides aren't allowed. Plenni is for the sad buggers, us, the 'clients'! Relax and enjoy.' She adds somewhat enthusiastically.

My eyes are drawn to the table and the four silver dishes, each one strategically placed in front of each of us. My dish has four silver plasters, 2 blue tablets and one beige tablet which resembled a large Victory V. Everyone had different combinations and some had different colours.

'Look at her! admirin' those goodies already.' quipped Andy. Gotta introduce yourself first.' he demanded.

'Oh, sorry, yes of course. I'm Helena, er number 2 I believe. My theme is leaving.' 'I added feeling quite embarrassed, like a school child who wants to join in, but feels inadequate. 'Emotional trauma or adjustment, something along those lines.' It sounded stupid. I knew that Barry would have something to say and he did.

'Ah trauma, similar difficulty to me then. Yes I see it now...' he began pompously.

'Get stuffed Barry, she's not an addictive wreck like you, or me for that matter. You want your goodies H?' he asked. 'Bugger off Barry.'

Barry simply glares at her a flicker of resentment in his eyes as he bites down on his huge Victory V.

'Any chance of a trade there H?' asks Andy 'Two blues for a silver, it's a crackin' deal!' he adds hopefully.

'Erm, what exactly are they?' I ask Shauna.

'Just shut it Andy, you grabbing bastard.' she snipes to Andy and then changes tone to talk to me. 'The flat one here,' she holds up the Victory V, 'that's your food supplement, just shove it in, no pleasure involved. The silver ones are like nicotine patches, quite a habit you had there. The blue ones are pure alcohol and we only get one each. That's your own daily ration and we don't trade!' she says glaring at Andy. I pick up the brown tablet and crunch it slowly, it tastes of yeast and barley with a hint of garlic. I meet Andy's smiley brown eyes.

'Not much taste there. By the by Helena who are your guides then?' he asks looking down and tugging his t shirt down over his smooth body.

'Why? Who are yours?' I ask cautiously.

'Richard Branson and Anneka Rice. Fantastic, what a combo. They should have married, what a team.'

'What enormous smiles their children would have.' I added.

'Brilliant!' adds Shauna, who giggles to herself as she administers her third silver plaster. 'Ah, that's better.' she sighs and closes her eyes, then adds, 'I've got Victoria Wood and Mel Gibson, they're mint.' I smile resisting a giggle as I try to imagine the advice they would give. I slap on a silver plaster and pure nicotine shoots through me, my heart thuds in a familiar manner and I breathe in deeply. Feeling confident I slap on a blue and the cosy glow of alcohol creeps warmly through my body. Lovely. I swear I can even taste a glimmer of Bacardi!

'And who has the mighty Helena selected to guide her through her traumatic adventure?' asks Andy cynically.

'Well,' I pause and slap on my last blue. God that's good. I hesitate, feeling the glorious effects of the alcohol, not slurring but almost.

'Tonight Mathew, I've chosen Jame Dudi Bench and the broody Alan Rickman.' I giggle at my mistake. Everyone laughs except Barry.

'Not my Alan, surely not, not sharing with you. I know he's popular, but really. Sharing with a light weight like you! My problems are real, complex, complicated ...'

'Oh for God's sake, shut it you miserable gobshite, leave her alone. It's only because you can't have a blue strip and get your booze fix. Anyway you've got to tell her your other choice Barry.' Shauna sneered.

A loud gong sounded and the beautiful blue backdrop faded to grey, the music stopped and the white lights were back.

'I refuse to respond to such a crass request.'

'I will then, you southern tart.' she stated. 'It's Esther, yep Esther Rantzen!!'

I exploded, the rush of alcohol and nicotine combined and escaped in the form of hysterical giggles.

'Esther and Alan, brilliant. Imagine them in bed together?' I laughed and so did everyone except Barry. The gong sounded again and I didn't want to leave. I could feel my heart pounding inside my head and the familiar feeling of panic. Shauna realised, I reached out to her. She grabbed my hand and squeezed it.

'See ya tomorrow, don't panic you'll get used to it.'

I slowly nodded and relaxed as the lights went whiter and then everything went black.

Theme music to *'That's life!'*

'I suppose you thought that was amusing.' sniped Alan Rickman in an unmistakably clipped tone. 'Esther and I between the sheets, discussing misshapen vegetables and their phallic qualities as she nibbles the nape of my neck! I'm pleased that I amuse you. The joke my dear is on you, *That's Death* would be far more appropriate!'

I open my eyes into the familiar white glare, feeling slightly hung over. I'm back in my suit facing the screen. Then I remember Plenni and smile as I remember Andy, Barry and Shauna. Suddenly, I feel less alone in my artificial world and wonder who my neighbours might be. The music clicks off and in the distance I can hear Flint muttering to himself about the dreaded first AA meeting he has to encounter with number 7, who I know now, is Barry.

'Yes it was.' chipped in Pink. 'I was delayed because of the tedious paperwork, seems quite endless.' she paused; I could imagine her collecting herself.

'Good morning Helena. I trust you enjoyed Plenni.' again more of a statement than a question. 'You may or may not have noticed that you are progressing, you'll see that the light on the first ball has now gone out. That's one issue resolved, you have understood and can now move forward.' The memory of the hospital stay fluttered across my mind merely brushing over me and I smiled. It had passed, had no impact, I understood. Freud may have had something after all.

'Yes you understand. It's resolved. This process is all about facing up to things and then letting go, so that you can move forward and...'

'And what, Dame Judi, what then, when I understand and move forward, what then? Do I win a prize, win my life back or just die all over again!'

I interrupt feeling irritated and annoyed like some observed guinea pig in a testing lab. 'What if I don't 'understand' the next one? I know my life; it's crammed with events, inconsistencies, anomalies what then?'

'Calm yourself Helena. It simply won't help to become agitated. You have not yet learnt patience. It is one of your lacks.'

'My lacks! Have you seen what's coming, I'm bound to have lacks, my life is crammed with lacks!' I raised my voice in frustration.

'I simply won't continue until you calm yourself. There it is. Admittedly you've had an 'interesting' time and that's why you're here. To work through it and resolve issues and to understand where your insecurities lie.' Again she paused and composed herself.

'I can send for Alan if you'd prefer, he is after all your second choice.'

I'd offended her. A bad move! Typical, typical of my reactive and sometimes destructive side. Stupid!

'No. No thank you. Sorry. I just don't want to fail, to let anyone down.' I explained.

'That trait in your character is how you got to be here. You have every chance. Some don't. We need to move on. My hands are tied regarding the future. Shall we continue?' she asked quietly.

'Yes. And I am grateful, really.' I added, feeling subdued by my lack of control.

'That's fine. Now then background information....'

I knew I was smiling as I imagined Dame Judi as M in the Bond films.

'Yes I was rather good.' She interrupted and I knew that she had forgiven my outburst. 'Moving along. You're now 19 years old. You're in the car, with your parents after successfully gaining a transfer down to Bristol to join your then fiancée. You're searching for a flat and are ambitiously starting your new job the following Monday. You don't know anybody in Bristol and have never been to the offices of the new job. You wanted to be closer to your fiancee, Jamie and this was the path you took. Need I go on? Of course not. I'm loading it now and you may use the fast forward where necessary.'

'Good God woman, it's hardly rocket science, just launch the damn thing!' Alan quipped in his usual curt manner.

'Flint, kindly return to Esther and try to show a modicum of empathy to 7.'

Then came the clicking of static and I was propelled through the screen straight into the back seat of a green Zephyr. Sitting next to your 19 year old self is somewhat unnerving.

I took at good look at myself, determined, focused, absolutely no doubt that I was doing the right thing.

Blue jeans, pink tea shirt, eyes fixed. My young face set, ready to take on the world. I looked confident and cock sure; this was a side of myself I hadn't seen for a very long time. Mum and Dad in the front, quietly discussing directions and the name of the guest house we would stay in. I watch myself kneading the white gold engagement ring with the tiny diamond and it filled me with excitement. I simply loved Jamie and that was and never has been under dispute. We pulled into a car park and Pink intervened.

'Recognise yourself?' she asked. 'Your confidence is quite amazing and your parents are extremely concerned, but supporting your new rather impulsive adventure. I believe it would be best to fast forward the flat hunting episode.'

'Let me intervene. Pink never really listens in the Tech sessions.' added Flint, 'it's only the tab key in shift Pink!'

With that he clicked off and the screen split into 4, flicking from one flat to another. I remembered the damp cellar flat in Redfield, the white monastic cell in Portishead, the filthy shared house in Downend and the box room which involved sharing a toilet between 8 people, in Yate. Most of all I marvelled at my parents' patience and concern as they climbed yet another set of badly carpeted stairs in yet another place which smelt of cabbage. We found nothing habitable or affordable. My then fiancée and I were quite young and a junior bank clerk's pay combined with a junior Navy Air Mechanic's pay meant that we were working in very close margins.

Finally, the flickering stopped.

'It's Sunday evening. You're now in the guest house, in your room with your parents.' Another click and I'm thrust into a small room with a single bed, electric fire, on a meter and a wooden table with one chair, where my dad sits crossing through the options. My mum and I sit on the bed exhausted and anxious. I look at myself, my confidence shaken. The light flickers in the small room. I can see in my 19 year old eyes, a look of fear as I know that my parents will have to leave and drive back to Manchester minus one daughter. A daughter who has no sense of direction, no idea where her new job is located and with no allies to guide her.

I shudder as I realise just how hard this must have been for mum and dad. I look at my face, still determined to begin my new life, find a place to stay and start a new job. My fiancée was sailing to Iceland, some War Games on an Aircraft Carrier, a three week tour.

Dad stands up, rattles the change in his pocket and lights a cigarette. This is it, I know that in 5 minutes they will be leaving. Mum pats my shoulder reassuringly. We have found some options that I can chase the following weekend. Dad stubs out his cigarette. I look at my face still resolved in my task, but equally terrified. We say our good byes and exchange hugs. We plan the phone calls for the following week. I walk to the main door of the guest house and then they are gone.

I return to my room, shaking and sit on my bed crest-fallen. Panic rushes through me. I count backwards from 10. Then a knock on the door, I spring up hope-fully. My mum is standing there. A reprieve, I thought to myself. Mum calmly reminded me to phone my sister and let her know that they had set off home to

Manchester. We re-say the good byes. The door closes again. The light flicks off and I fumble for the change to put in the meter. It suddenly dawns on me that I'm in a huge Southern city, I have never even visited, preparing to start a new job based in a guest house on the Clifton Downs!

The screen flicks and I'm sat in the bath, sobbing my heart out and wondering what the hell I have done. I look at my tear stained face and now realise that this was the beginning of a journey when I had to learn to be alone. This would be echoed throughout my life, fortunately for me with the tremendous support of my family.

I remember finding my way to work and beginning my new job. A Northerner in a very Southern environment. My fiancée and I married during the Falklands conflict.

The screen flickered and went black.

'Do you see your theme taking shape Helena?' asked Pink as the lights flashed back on. I sighed and nodded. Shell shocked and tired. 'I'll auto infuse. Just relax and drift.'

I closed my eyes and could hear the faint strains of *In the Navy* by the Village People, which I used to detest. I knew it was the work of Flint and smiled. Secretly pleased he was watching over me.

Stairway to heaven
Led Zeppelin

I groaned. I really didn't want to wake up. I forced my eyes tightly shut against what I knew would be the glaring white light and the dreaded big screen. Memories of Bristol fluttered through my mind. This was hard, reliving a past. Having vague memories of what was to come, not wanting to face them. I preferred the grey faded version in my mind to the full technicolour version of reality. Worst of all I was beginning to pull together the threads of my theme and it was painful. Of course this was only the beginning. I shuddered, clinging onto the cosy darkness of oblivion.

'We could jump start her with the auto node!' said Flint. I could hear the underlying enthusiasm in his voice.

'Really Flint. Do you have even the slightest modicum of empathy? I've never been convinced that this if the right line of work for you. *Die Hard* and *Robin Hood* hardly boosts one's confidence!' retorted Pink.

'And I suppose your roles in *A Fine Romance* and *Ladies in Lavender* make you feel superior!' he clips back.

'Just stop!' I shout. 'Give me some space, please.'

'The purple booster would do the trick. The pain is minimal. I used it on 7. Highly amusing. He did need to change his suit, but...'

'Flint! Desist. I do realise that for some reason Helena did request you, but... .'

'Stop! Both of you!!' I shouted. 'It's hard work this post death analysis crap! Just put me on snooze! Like you did before!... Please!' I added.

'The girl does not deserve Plenni Pink.' He paused with perfect timing. 'You do realise, my dear Helena, that should you miss Plenni you go straight to your next ball.' He paused. 'Anyway, I have bigger fish to fry, Esther takes over with her consumer advice when I'm not there!'

A click and he was gone. I managed a slight grin.

'Now then Helena it is time for Plenni.' her voice softening. 'Would you care to join the others?'

I groaned and then remembered the goodies on offer and Shauna. I begrudgingly opened my eyes.

'That's better. Plenni will provide some respite.'

A switch clicked. I was free from the dreaded suit – paradise. I was sat at the table at the same place. This time the backdrop was pink with a different selection of whirring planets. There was music playing faintly, it sounded like an 80's compilation. I got my bearings and looked around, everyone was there.

'Hiya H, thought you weren't bloody coming!' boomed Shauna. It was good to see her.

'Good day my dear. Nice of you to join us. A little tardy, but then you are a newcomer.' stated Barry rather condescendingly...

'Alright then?' nodded Andy. I shrugged my shoulders. Andy and Barry then continued a somewhat heated discussion about football versus rugby.

'Borin' tossers.' Shauna grinned and pulled my chair nearer to hers. 'You OK kiddah?' she asked, genuine concern in her stark blue eyes. I crunched on my Victory V and slapped on silver, feeling almost instant relief. I sighed and patted her arm.

'How do you cope?' I asked. 'What the hell is going on? It's all so weird and fuckin' strange!!'

'Slow down H.' she paused. 'Here have yer blue.' I obeyed. It immediately took the edge off. I sighed, looking down at my feet and wondering how they looked so real.

'I can't answer all your questions. I dunno myself. I'm only on ball 4! Yeah, it's shit. Most of it a blur, can't soddin well remember and would rather not! But, it's like Mel said..'

'Mel Gibson.' I added hesitantly.

'Yeah, it's like Mel said, we must be here for a bloody good reason. God he's lovely, he'd be a good enough reason for me. Couldn't you just!! I can't believe it me havin' a natter with Mel.'

I laughed partly through relief.

'Victoria, yeah, Victoria Wood, she's mint, just pulls me through and stops me feelin' like a dick.' She paused. 'Jesus you picked a bleedin' hard case. Rickman! Are you a bloody sadist or summat?'

I smiled. 'He's tough. I admit. But I like him and his voice is so...'

'Sexy! Yeah I know. You mean he's a sarky bastard!'

'Well, yes, but he's funny and... .'

We were interrupted.

'You're quite simply a Welsh, sheep obsessed bastard Andrew!!' shouted Barry.

'English tosser. Jumped up gobshite!!' retorted Andy.

The chairs shrieked on the polished floor as they both wrenched them sideways and sat back to back.

'Boys and fuckin' sport!!' shouted Shauna. 'No bleedin' surprise! Pack it in you silly bastards!' No one moved. I squirmed in my chair, disliking the confrontation. Shauna noticed. 'You're upsetting H. Come on lads! This is our time, away from that!' her voice trembled. 'Look we'll be energized, put back in the collective! Come on!'

I was surprised by her passion.

'Fuck it! Come on Barry, tell us about culture, the high life, Andy tell us about your best con, the stakes... Come on!!'

Shauna really did need Plenni, I realised, more than most of us. Her head went down.

A few moments later, Barry tapped Andy on the shoulder.

'OK, old man.' Andy shrugged and they elbowed each other like school boys and turned their chairs around.

Shauna responded. 'Fuckin' great lads! Slap on those plasters my fellow guinea pigs and let's talk!'

We all obeyed willingly with whatever we had left.

'So Helena, has Dame Judi lost her rag with the moody Rickman yet?' inquired Barry with a raised eyebrow. I smiled.

'She keeps him in his place.' I said.

'Branson's great!' added Andy. 'Him and Annie never row! Well except the one time.' He went quiet.

'Jesus Andy, spill the fuckin' beans, we're gaggin' to know!!' enthused Shauna.

'Well it's not that interestin' really.' He paused. 'Well OK then. It was about one of my dodgy take over bids.

All underhand, you know. Involved in the stock market, lies and deceit, the usual, but there it is. Branson got angry, called me names, even called me a tosser he did!'

'Hold on there Andrew! Richard Branson dropped his guard, stopped the smilieness and called you a tosser!!' responded Barry. He chuckled.

'Bloody fantastic! I mean Branson losing control old chap, not you!' he added. 'What did the fair Anneka do?' he asked.

'She said she'd never heard anything like it! And despite my underhanded deceit and money grabbin' nature, she was sure that Richard wasn't lily white and she suggested that he may have been a scheming business man along the way! Richard went berserk!! He told her that mere celebrities, sponsored by advertising were ten a penny and would never be able to hold their heads up in the business world!' he paused and crunched thoughtfully on his Victory V.

We all gasped, imaging the scene.

'They didn't speak for 2 days. Not a word! Then Hopkins intervened. Shauna and Barry gasped. There was silence.

'Hopkins? 'I asked. No-one responded.

'Hopkins, as in Mary Hopkins, long blond hair, guitar, Eurovision. Strange choice for anyone.' I added.

Shauna was unable to control herself. She was bent over double. Andy chuckled to himself, even Barry let out an upper class snort.

'My dear Helena you are priceless.' He guffawed.

'What?' I asked innocently.

'HE, is revered and respected, the omniscient narrator of this bizarre farce! He makes all the decisions, decides on our futures, my dear girl, we are of course referring to the one and only ANTHONY HOPKINS!' he stated and then laughed to himself. Shauna had tears trickling down her face and kept banging her clenched fist on the table. Andy was still chuckling. I smile, rubbed my forehead and rubbed my fingers across my mouth before giggling away to myself. Shauna slapped me on the back and gave my arm a tight squeeze.

Gradually, we all calmed down, enjoying the relief from the break in the tension. Barry began humming *Knock knock, who's there* and we all began laughing again. The lights flickered and the backdrop faded.

'You are mint!' exclaimed Shauna. 'Great Plenni! What do you say boys, are the girls the best fuckin' laughter makers or what?'

'Good story Andy,' drawled Barry, 'even if it was for all the wrong reasons!' Praise indeed from the upper crust Barry. Andy grinned and put his head down in an attempt at bashfulness.

'Right, come on sad bastards. As we're dead already, hands in the middle of the table, that's right!' We all obeyed. 'Now shout YEAH!'

We all did, a second before the clicking and static shot us back into our pods. I'm sure I heard the distant chuckle of my beloved Flint before grinning to myself and falling into a dreamless sleep without speaking to either of my Guides. Sweet release!

Don't leave me this way
The Communards

I woke up smiling, as if I'd had a great night out on the town. I loved this record and for a moment, just a moment, I never considered its relevance. Click, buzz, a flicker of static and I was back in the spotlight. But somehow I felt better equipped, less drained, ready to face the surreal nightmare of my day/night.

'Flint!' cut in Pink.

'Always my pleasure.' he responded dryly and the music faded away into the distance.

'Good morning Helena. How lovely to see you awake.'

'They hit the sound bar at Plenni last night.' interrupted Flint.

'What?' I asked, smothering a yawn.

'Oh, I see.' said Pink.

'You were extremely lucky my dear girl that I was on duty and decided not to alert the panel,' he paused. 'Or bleep Hopkins.'

He knew!! I knew he knew. But how? They weren't supposed to listen in, to be involved in our private world. It was supposed to be our time, our space.

'Stop that bleating woman!' Flint boomed into my head. 'For God's sake if the sound level goes above regulation because of raised voices or fighting, then a sensor quite simply triggers an alarm and the duty manager uses his discretion, i.e. me! Remember, my dear, sweet Helena that some of our 'guests' can become violent. It can get quite ugly. Some of our clientele become desperate, repressed memories and missed opportunities can unleash bitterness, aggression enhanced by alcohol, it can be a dangerous cocktail.'

'So you do listen!!' I shouted. 'That's why you played the theme from *That's Life* when I first came!'

'No, well yes, he did. At that stage we probably shouldn't have ...'

'We? You mean you all do it!! Dear God. I never thought that *you* would stoop that low!'

'It's comforting to know that you obviously didn't think it beneath me!' sneered Flint.

'Anyway,' interrupted Pink quietly. ' Let's not waste time, there's a mountain of things to do.' Pink was rattled, I could tell, but there was no way I was going to let this drop.

'Is there no privacy in this hell hole!!? You're both in my head ALL day and then even in the scrap of respite we get from this personal intrusion, which we are told is private, then you're THERE as well!!' I was shouting and I knew it.

'Calm yourself Helena.' asserted Flint. 'The regulations are there for your own protection. Much as I hate to leave, I simply must dash. I'll leave her in your capable hands Pink, 7 needs me.' and with that Flint clicked off.

'Right, now Helena, no time to dwell on the past. Shall we ...' I interjected.

'No time to dwell on the past!!! You don't seem to mind dwelling on **my** past!!! Wouldn't you say that's double standards?'

Pink coughed. 'I really don't see the point of spending any more time on this and you *will* miss your slot if we do and that's serious Helena. It is, of course your choice.' she added quietly.

'Choice!' I responded, raising my voice again. 'My 'choice' would be to go home, to wake up in my own bed and carry on with my life rather than my death. Is that a choice!! ?'

Suddenly, the lights dipped, the screen flicked off and I was aware that a third party was now involved.

'Wait!' Pink raised her voice clearly addressing someone other than me. 'She doesn't understand, she's new.' I could hear the panic in her voice.

'Helena, panel can override me, shut you down, end your chances. There is no more time!'

Oh my God, I thought to myself. This was worse than *Big Brother*. I gulped. Even this tedious existence was better than finality, the ultimate closure.

'Pink? Are you there?' I asked timidly. 'I'm sorry, I just got so annoyed at Flint listening in and ....Can we continue? Are we allowed to carry on?'

'Yes, at least I think so, wait a moment and well; try not to think.'

I imagined the brick wall again and a ticking clock.

More clicking, then the lights were restored and the screen flickered into life.

'Thank you.' I said quietly.

'That was close.' said Flint from a distance.

'That must never happen again Helena - the sensors here are very advanced and can pick up anxiety and heightened emotion. Not everyone can deal with dipping back into their past lives especially as we are focusing on the less pleasant incidents. Consider that your last chance. They can and will pull the plug and there's nothing that Flint and I can do to reverse that process once it begins.'

'I understand. Sorry I lost my temper.'

I could hear the strains of *Sorry seems to be the hardest word* by Elton John in the background, but chose to keep this to myself in case Pink wasn't privvy to it.

'I've loaded the third ball, I'm afraid it's rather like the edited highlights of a film, there was a lot to fit in.'

'That's fine.' I said meekly.

'You're in Bristol, stood in a queue with your fiancé Jamie in a chip shop I believe. You are both watching a television behind the counter.' My stomach lurched as I instantly remembered. This one I didn't want to re-live.

The TV flickered innocently, unaware of the profundity of the message it relayed. It was the very first announcement by the sickeningly familiar face of John Nott, the Secretary of State for Defence. It was May 1982. Then came the announcement that war against the Falklands had begun. They were cut-ins of Margaret Thatcher with her patronising expression as she condescendingly delivered the forthcoming death sentences to all branches of the Armed services. I watched from the outside and inside at the same time, noting the tight grip of our hands as the chips fried and the mushy peas bubbled.

Then the screen changed again. All three of us were mounting the stairs, as Jamie banged the timer switches and we made our way up to the newly rented flat. The flat that we had only just moved into that week, so that we could be together. The chips discarded, I watched our young faces heavy with the impact of the news, whitened by the implications of the newly entered war. I watched my face crumple as I fell onto Jamie's broad shoulders that had promised me protection and togetherness. Tears filled my eyes and I wanted to go back to the pod.

'Stay there Helena.' demanded Pink.

'Take me back, please take me back! It's too hard!!' I begged.

Jamie wiped my tears and hugged me tightly as my body was sobbed with pain.

Thank God. The screen flickered and I was back in the stark homeland of my pod. I shuddered and wiped the tears from my eyes. My emotions were flowing like volcanic ash, searing my insides, fired by my hatred of the Navy. I now realised that it was the powerlessness I hated, the lack of control. I began to feel the familiar chill creeping through my body. I now knew what came next, the shaking. I drew my feet up to my stomach in preparation for the shock and devastating fear that would ensue. I knew the routine, very well. As I rocked myself in my artificial world, it suddenly dawned on me that this had been the beginning. Much of my future life would be shaped by these moments and the fuelling of insecurity that always followed.

'Plenni please?' I asked despairingly.

'I'm sorry Helena, you see that wasn't everything, there's more. We pulled you back to give you some respite. You may feel more comfortable with the next one.' said Pink in her sensible, reassuring manner.

This was hard, very hard. I had once loved this man, and then taught myself not to. It had taken me a very very long time. It was passed. I had moved on.

'Not quite.' snipped Pink. 'You see you haven't moved on not completely. This part of your life was when you established certain aspects of your behaviour that stayed with you and...'

'Pink, keep out of my head! Please! Stop analysing me!' I shrieked.

'Helena, calm yourself. I have to warn you that the window is closing and Plenni will no longer be an option if you miss this.'

I sighed deeply.

'Do it.' I said resignedly, through gritted teeth.

I was back. Jamie was sat on the old settee, which was covered in a cream throw to hide its shabbiness. The pale blue, faded check curtains were drawn across the skylight window. It was the next morning. Jamie had his head in his hands. He'd missed his ship's departure.

I lay in the darkened bedroom crippled with the worst migraine I have ever had. My speech was slurred and delayed and I had flickering vision through one eye. Half of my body was paralysed and my head pounded with sickening pain. Black shadows surrounded swollen eyes as I sobbed in the darkness. Jamie had looked after me, when the hysterics had calmed and sheer desperation took over. I looked at this scene with such knowing and the dread of the inevitable punishment for Jamie which would ensue. A bang on the door signalled the promptness of the 'bastard' navy's intrusion. We had no telephone. A policeman stood at the door. He was pleasant enough of course, 'Just doin' my job love, is all.' he told me cheerily in a thick Bristolian accent as he led Jamie away to face his punishment. I looked across at the shuddering heap he had left behind. My young tear stained face and arms crossed against my ribs as if hugging the pain. Then I noticed it. It was only subtle and very fast. I recognised it immediately, but it was the first time that I'd seen it from the outside. It was a look of vulnerability, a flicker. A piercing stab of insecurity and then came the worst bit. The dead pan stunned mask. I have felt this a thousand times on the inside, but never seen the process as it happens. It was the birth of a blueprint, a way of reacting, which would recur and I could see it now. The worst thing of all was that 25 years on I could still go into this kind of debilitating shock.

I sighed and began aching with the realisation, I was only beginning to understand the impact and damage which my theme of 'Leaving' had played throughout my life. I understood why I had to see it. The screen crackled.

'Are you alright my dear? ' asked Pink.

I cleared my throat.

'It went down you know, the ship that Jamie missed, The Atlantic Conveyor. It went down with all his kit on it.' I told Pink in a strange automaton's voice.

'Yes, I know.' Pink softened her tone.

'He went with the next ship 7 days after we were married. There was a cease fire on our wedding day 15th June 1982, but he still left. People leave don't they Pink. You know what happened after this, don't you?' a sob which seemed to come from my stomach interrupted me.

'People leave don't they?'

'Put the girl out Pink! Her vitals are reading too low!' interrupted Flint.

'Pink! Her blood pressure's dropping!' he added panicking.

The familiar feeling of cold creeping through me and the nausea. I desperately wanted alcohol and nicotine.

'Plenni! Let me go to Plenni please!' I shouted.

'There's no chance.' snapped Flint.

A black dot came towards me, growing larger and larger, I was being switched off. Everything went black.

Heaven can wait.
Meatloaf

M y head pounded in time with the music – a little early for Meatloaf even in my book.

'It could have been '*Bat out of hell*' instead.' interrupted Rickman.

I yawned and shuddered as I remembered the latest 'Leavings' instalment.

'Good Morning Helena.' said Dame Judi in a brusque, Mary Poppinesque fashion. 'Now there really isn't any time to spare, Alan and I would hate you to miss this particular Plenni.'

I groaned, fearing yet another soul searching challenge.

'Well if that's her attitude Pink...' snarled Alan. 'Perhaps Cinders will miss the ball.'

'What? I mean what's special today. I mean I love Plenni but..'

'Right then, are you ready? OK Pink.'

'I feel that it would be pertinent to just warn you Helena, after all Flint it is 7's choice.'

'His choice?' I became even more interested.

'Don't spoil it woman!' gnarled Flint.

'I will just say that it's 7's last Plenni. Now then are you ready Helena?' Pink added.

For once I felt an air of anticipation heightened by my guide's conversation. I loved Plenni of course and it would be...'

'Kindly stop your blithering woman, you're interfering with the signal!' snipped Alan.

A flash and a flicker and then I was there. I could hear sounds of muffled laughter and Shauna's unmistakable voice as I came to.

We were in the same room as normal, more guffaws and loud music, but something felt very different. I noticed that two of the walls were now mirrored and the lighting seemed more sophisticated. I felt strange, stranger than usual. I shrugged and shook my head. That's when I noticed that there was definitely something wrong with my hair and I also seemed to be sporting a heavy coat of make-up. My hand went automatically to my face. I appeared to be coated in glossy lipstick and thick lashes of mascara which made me feel like I was looking at the world through bars. I touched my hair, a lacquered, stiff affair, which didn't move when I moved my head. I looked down to my feet which were housed in white strappy sandals that matched the white dress. A tight bodice and pleated white skirt and no tights I noticed, which begged the question of who dressed me! I swivelled my chair around and caught my reflection in one of the mirrors. I gasped. I was donned in a ghastly Marilyn Monroe outfit. I immediately stood up and checked my tummy and bottom in the mirror. I am a girl after all. I shook my blonde hair which refused to move and seemed plastered to my head. I sat down feeling slightly giddy. I shrugged my shoulders and then began to look around for my fellow guests. I could see the backs of 3 people, all dressed in equally bizarre outfits. Their voices raised as they argued over the next record. The first back I examined was reasonably easy to recognise, top hat and tails, very striking. Top hat was stood next to a girl, Shauna I presumed who wore a very tailored black dress, long black gloves and her hair styled into an elegant bun. I was even jealous of her outfit and figure just looking at her from the back! Next a bit of a puzzler, a man in black leather trousers and a white flouncy shirt. I began to giggle to myself this was going to be fun. The sound of The Drifters *Saturday Night at the Movies* came on, as one by one they turned toward me.

Firstly, Barry who looked immaculate in his shiny black top hat, black jacket and trousers, gleaming shoes, pristine white handkerchief in his breast pocket and black brass tipped stick which he expertly bounced down onto the floor and then caught before dancing and tapping his way across the room. How brilliant ! I was delighted as he rolled his top hat down his arm and bent from the waist to kiss my hand. Excellent!!! Barry made a brilliant Fred Astaire!

'Good evening Marilyn.' he crooned and sat down beside me. 'Welcome to my evening bash, my leaving soiree.' he added as he slapped on a blue patch. Oh NO,

'But Barry ..!'

'I'm allowed one tonight dear Marilyn, as it's the end of the line so to speak.' he grinned weakly at me. Then he slapped on his patch and old Fred was back. His eyes lit up with excitement as the blue patch kicked in. He half closed his eyes and sighed, a deep sigh almost the same sigh you give after meeting a long lost friend. In a way this was exactly the same thing for Barry.

'Marvellous!' he exclaimed. 'Bloody marvellous!!.'

He sighed again and then burst into life.

'Audrey darling do join us.'

I gasped. Of course Audrey Hepburn/Shauna and she looked fantastic.

Shauna turned elegantly and really did look the part. Her dress was beautifully tailored, a diamond necklace hugged her neck and matched the diamond clip which had been clipped at the base of her fringe. The long black silky gloves gave her a sexy look as she smoothed them delicately up her arms. She glided slowly across the floor, subtly swinging her hips as she took tiny steps. She sat down knees together and then regally slanted to one side as she positively beamed at me across the table.

'Wow! You look amazing!!' I said as Fred smiled at her.

Her face was delicately made up, enhanced by the diamond ear rings. The deep red lipstick was subtle and her eyes shone under well curled lashes.

'Honestly Shauna you really do look just like her, it's brilliant!' I couldn't get over the transformation.

'Alright cocker?' she asked smiling, clearly delighted with her outfit.

'Don't scrub up too bad for bloody rejects trapped in the *twilight zone* do we?' she asked, the guttural vowels ever so slightly shattering the illusion. A bit like when Kate Moss did the exact same, a beautiful image destroyed with a simple phrase - never had *getting the Landon look* cost so dear.

'Enough Audrey!' demanded Barry. 'This is my party.' he added, then softening his tone. 'Please, if you would, for me?' he almost pleaded. Shauna rose to the occasion admirably.

'I will at once my dear.' she purred sexily recrossing her legs. 'The night is yet young. Do ask our last guest to join us.'

Fred grinned delighted by her efforts.

'Why of course my dear.' he added. I looked across toward Andy's back still unaware as to his new identity. Andy turned around on queue and Shauna and I both collapsed across the table grabbing hands and howling with laughter. Andy was quite a convincing Tom Jones, from a distance, until that is he began to clomp across the room toward us. His gold medallion catching the disco lights making patterns on his flouncy white shirt. The black leather trousers, a tad too tight causing him to stop half way across the dance floor and rearrange himself. This added to the hilarity and he was clearly none too pleased. His new found black curly hair even glistened characteristically with sweat. He grabbed the side of the chair as he leant backwards attempting to sit down without bending. After a few moments he jerked violently into his seat.

'Fuck off the lotta you!' he almost shouted in embarrassment. Barry was laughing discreetly beneath his white glove. Andy's eyes darkened and we all attempted to suppress our mirth.

'What the 'ell is goin on?' demanded Andy angrily.

Shauna was now biting her fingers in an attempt at controlling herself.

'Quite simply my friends it's my party, my leaving party, my night and my choice. I selected your outfits and have managed to acquire a generous supply of patches for my final evening before going who knows where.'

Religiously we all slapped on our patches, eager to continue in an escapist mode.

'Thanks a fuckin' bunch Barry. You all glammed up for the night and me trussed up like an ageing sex bomb!' he pulled out a white hankie and mopped his brow. 'Not surprised he sweats in these bleedin' trousers!' at which point he began adjusting his crotch and Shauna and I lost it altogether.

'Thank you everyone! Mock the Welshie, bloody great!'

I could see that Andy was genuinely upset and calmed myself quickly, wanting everyone to have a good time.

'You do look the part Andy, really it is a great costume and you're a great sport. Look at me, I look like a transvestite on heat!'

His mouth broke into a smile.

'No, no, ah well you do look erm ..'

'I know.' I interrupted. I began laughing as we looked over to the mirrors.

'Top party,' added Shauna. 'We all look like misfits from *Stars in your eyes*.' Everyone laughed.

'Now then Marilyn, give us a twirl and then we're all in character.' demanded Andy. I bowed my head shyly, knowing it was only fair. I slapped on a patch and responded to the chanting group. I took a deep breath and walked rather racily over to the mirrors. I twirled enjoying the flair of my pleated white skirt, and then bobbed down, pouted and held my white dress above my thighs imitating the famous pose. Everyone clapped in time with the music and it felt great to join in. I returned to the table my cheeks slightly flushed.

'It's a frightfully good party.' gushed Audrey as I reclaimed my seat.

'OK double patches for my friends before we dance, I've been allowed to preset a song each, but we all dance.' and we all obeyed.

It was a brilliant night, enhanced by double patches but everyone joined in. Tom Jones danced raunchily to *It's not unusual*, Fred danced beautifully to *Top Hat and Tails*, Audrey danced divinely to *Breakfast at Tiffany's* and I posed my way through *I wanna be loved by you*. We finished off with Barry's choice *My Way*. The lights flickered which meant we had to go. We stood holding hands in a circle.

'Good night dear friends. Good luck to you. Enough said.'

He shook Andy's hand, managing half a man hug, but not quite. He gently hugged Shauna and winked reassuringly at her. Silencing her lips with his finger. He put his arm around my shoulder and whispered something quite strange in my ear.

'Your theme is leaving, this is my last night Helena. Could we be part of your story? It's a puzzle. Work it out, I think there is a way.'

As we clung together in group hug all jumping together to the strains of *Come on Eileen*. The thought triggered something in my head. I made myself store it, it was too dangerous, they would pick it up. One last hug and the room went black as we were transported back to our pods after a brilliant night. How clever of Barry to have distracted us from the seriousness of his last night in such an inventive way! Sleep now and happy dreams I hope.

Don't fear the Reaper
Blue Oyster Cult

For the first time in a long time, I woke up smiling. This was not due to Flint's black sense of humour, it was the after glow from last night's Plenni. The party was excellent and ended on such a high note when it could easily have been a morbid, sombre affair. I felt a strange feeling of relief which must have been due to the release of tension. A sad situation had been made so much easier and wonderfully enjoyable by using a bit of imagination. I sighed contentedly and closed my eyes for a moment. The golden glow of the mood was shattered as my mind decided to up load an image of a brick wall, the brick wall from '*Village of the damned*' used to stop the children from reading the hero's mind, so that he could blow up the building and destroy them. I shook myself awake and tried to pull this vital memory to the forefront of my mind after filing it so cleverly away in my head. Then I heard Barry's voice again, 'Work it out Helena, there has to be a way!'

This was not the time to be working anything out, I was far too exposed here in my pod, with Flint and Pink bobbing in and out of my head uninvited. I focused on controlling the memory so that it didn't trigger the detail. I closed my eyes and visualised the wall removing one of the bricks which was recognisable as it had a chipped corner. I forced the memory behind the wall and replaced the brick, reassuring myself that I was in total control and it had gone. I tapped my leg impatiently through my suit and started to hum *It's not unusual* to myself. Flint immediately interrupted,

'Very tuneful Helena.' Flint interrupted. 'Pink, it's time to tell Helena about the blocker.' he ordered. 'I've got the 'new one' to induct. He didn't select me, but his damn guide's not online yet. Mind you he didn't select Pink either.'

I could tell from his familiar snarly tone that he didn't suspect anything untoward or he would have definitely been questioning me by now.

'I have the pleasure of introducing 'Brian' and his OCD (obsessive compulsive disorder) to life as he doesn't know it. How quaint. Thinks he's unique. Pah!' with that there was a click and then he was gone. I sighed; things were getting progressively weirder, if that was possible. Thank God for Plenni, without it the whole thing would have been too intense and desperately lonely.

'Helena, good morning my dear.' bustled Pink. 'Now then it's time to concentrate as we have much to do. Today we will be removing the blocker of course. I know that Flint ran through that with you so we can make up some time and... .'

'Flint ran through it like this,' I interrupted, 'Pink will tell you about the blocker' and then he buggered off to Brian the new OCD guy.'

'I totally despair. He's broken the rules by telling you about Brian's erm difficulty and in addition he chooses to shirk his responsibilities and leave it to me. I am running more clients than he is!' Pink seemed tired and a little melancholy. She paused, inhaled and exhaled through her mouth which I could imagine seeing her do and then carried on stoically. I shuddered wondering what was in store for me now, the old fear begin to creep through me.

'Let me explain.' comforted Pink in her reassuring matronly voice. 'It's quite straightforward. You see when our new clients arrive we want them to really concentrate on the events in their lives that they are viewing and this is almost certainly more effective if there are no distractions. Therefore we block certain aspects or memories of people or relatives until they progress and then we reintroduce them or as Flint puts it, *lift the blocker*. It is the fairest thing to do as blurring the experience with memories and projected opinions dilutes the process.' she paused.

'I see.' I said wondering nervously who the hell they had blocked for me. I tried to concentrate and will these missing people back into my mind. It was hopeless. The blocker was obviously highly successful at living up to its name. 'And my blocker, could you tell me before you remove it who or what you've blocked?' I asked.

'Yes, we did have a very long meeting with Panel about this. Anyway the outcome was that it was better to inform the client, but only if they asked. It can be rather a shock, I'm afraid. Well, with you Helena we blocked your children, now brace yourself while I lift it.'

I was shocked. Furious more like.

'You blocked my children!! How cruel. How bloody cruel. You had no right!' I was angry and appalled that I hadn't over ridden it in some way. What sort of a mother was I? You can't forget you have children.

Oh God what if the next instalment showed my failure as a parent and…

'Stop it Helena.' Pink said in a matter of fact voice. 'You're overreacting and it won't help. We do this to all our clients. Now calm down for goodness sake and stop trying to remember, it won't work. It's called a blocker for a reason.'

The lights flickered. Flint's voice cut in.

'You should be more direct Pink!' criticised Flint. 'No room or time for lengthy discussions. Is she finally ready or shouldn't I ask?'

'I am here you know. You talk about me as if I wasn't here, which is very rude considering that you have no qualms about dipping in and out of my mind! ' I added. 'And I am, most definitely, ready.'

The light in the room turned violet and a sparkly 3 D diamond appeared on the screen in front of me. I felt strange and light headed, the feeling you get just before a migraine attack. Then a warm glow filled me which was delicious like drinking hot milky cocoa on a freezing cold day. There was a nauseating clicking sound in my head which only lasted for a few seconds. My eyes flickered momentarily as the light in my room turned to a golden yellow. Then, they were there! Images of my two little girls zapped straight into my head. They were both laughing and giggling as they ran across a field. My stomach clenched as memories of their physical birth came back to me.

'They'll stay at this age for now Helena and continue to grow older as you do.'

I smiled and felt contented, I hadn't forgotten them. How could anyone forget them I thought as I watched their whoops of delight as Jamie chased them around pretending to be a monster. My love for my girls flooded through me. They were quite simply, just beautiful. They began climbing a gate and with Jamie's help all three were sat on the top bar swinging their legs. They all smiled and waved happily. Then the sun caught their eyes, their father's eyes looking back at me. I felt very uncomfortable.

'Pink she's cross patching. Move her on!' said Flint hurriedly.

'What the hell's cross patching? 'I asked irritably.

'It's when the future memories seep through the blocker into the past and it ruins your experience.'

'I have it under control Flint.' said Pink firmly. 'I know it's a shock but we have to move on Helena.' She paused.

'You're now living in Kingswood in Bristol in a nice 3 bedroom semi with the girls. Jamie has a good job after leaving the Navy as you agreed before you had children. Jamie has gone away to a convention in Manchester and is ironically staying with your parents for a few nights.'

I swallowed and got a salty taste in my mouth which you do when you're going to be sick.

The screen crackled and then I was thrust into my bedroom with two extra mounds in my bed, one upside down and wriggling and the other fast asleep. Jamie kissed me as he left for the long drive ahead. I looked younger, but strained around the eyes. My oldest daughter Sammy was shrieking as she did her caterpillar impression and the youngest Ellen woke with a smile and a yawn. At 14 months of age she was still an absolute delight, she ate, slept, laughed and was genuinely happy with her lot. Her blue green eyes twinkled when she giggled and auburn baby hair framed a pretty little face. Sammy was the big sister, always active and at 3 years of age the mischievous spark in her eyes had grown stronger. She was an early walker, talker and a strong character who had often had her Papa and Daddy wrapped around her little finger. Silky white strips of blonde hair had eventually covered the baby baldness and together with crystal blue eyes, she often appeared angelic.

After a brief tickling game, we all donned our dressing gowns and went downstairs. Milk, toast and cartoons completed the breakfast ritual. I looked at myself, I seemed happy enough. Motherhood hadn't come easily, but my love for my daughters was overwhelming. I seemed busy and focused. There was an underlying confidence which I knew was about to be knocked.

'Well done Helena, you're getting rather good at this.' interrupted Pink.

I knew what she meant as I was beginning to see the way that I had changed and more to the point, I was beginning to find a new way of responding to crisis and stress. My younger years had become the playing fields for a behaviour pattern, that would become almost automatic.

I watched myself changing the girls, washing their hands and faces under great protest and gently brushing their fine baby hair. I smiled in the past and present at the same time, only in the past it was followed by a small sigh and a faraway look. There it was the uncertainty, the tiny chip in my confidence that would lead to an almighty crack.

My past and present self both jumped slightly as the letter box rattled noisily due to the catch being stiff. The familiar noise was like a starting gun at a horse race and both of the girls were away. Sammy got a head start of course and grabbed the letters in her tiny hands as Ellen attempted to pull one from her. Sammy then turned smiling wickedly and promptly played Postman Pat and posted all the letters back through the letter box. Ellen shrieked with delight and Sammy chuckled to herself.

'All gone.' she added, holding her hands in the air.

As I looked back on this moment I froze and tried to will my 23 year old self to just leave the damn letters, remain in ignorance for a little while longer. Stupid avoidance tactics, I chastened myself sternly. So I had to watch myself prop open the door with my foot so that Sammy didn't slam it and lock me out and collect the scattered post. I watched myself pick up Ellen and follow Sammy in to sit at the table. I tried to will my younger self to leave those blessed letters as nothing would be the same again.

There were 5 letters, two circulars and 3 from banks I had never heard of. All three were addressed to Jamie!

I looked at my young face whiten and my body stiffen, I could almost hear the blood pounding in my ears across the years. I walked around the room cuddling Ellen and listening distantly to Sammy's 6 verse rendition of Humpty Dumpty, most of it improvised so that he had many more injuries. My older version of me would never have hesitated, I would have ripped the envelopes open at once. But Helena, I reminded myself, at this time did not know. Jamie's late nights and furtive behaviour had been a real worry and I had my suspicions. Deep down I had been worrying and narrowed it down to one of 3 things. My dad had already listed them for me months before when Jamie's behaviour had changed. It could have been an affair, drugs or gambling. None of which I was ready to face. The bank letters pointed quite clearly to the latter. After all the questions, all the arguments and all the lies, proof now lay before me in the sickening daylight. My young hands shook as I ripped the statements open. I looked at my horrified face as shock set in. Jamie owed thousands of pounds, over £8000 and this was 1988. I watched myself phone my parents, desperate for support and some answers. My perfect little family and our future now seemed shattered.

'We've decided to pull you out now Helena.' Pink piped up as the screen went dead. 'Quite enough for one day. You are beginning to recognise things and put together not just the events, but the way these events have shaped you.'

'Yes, I see.' I added absentmindedly. 'It's all too horrible to watch. But I am beginning to see the pattern and the way that I respond to shock is taking root. I feel tired now Pink. I'm glad you pulled me out. I know the next bit and I want to see it with fresh eyes.'

'Good girl, that's the spirit. You're doing very well. Time for rest.'

Everything went black.

Money
Pink Floyd

I awoke slowly to the sound of the jingling cash registers from *Money,* how tactless I thought to myself. Flint's idea of a joke no doubt. My stomach tightened as the sickening re-enactment of my introduction to gambling debts kicked in. As if to compensate a warm rush flowed through me as images of my babies flickered through my head. I wanted to push the memory forward and see the girls as they must be now. It was impossible, the blocker was total, and no amount of effort or directed concentration would budge it. I tried all the techniques that usually proved successful, going through the alphabet, using bizarre word association and flicking quickly from one image to another to try and trick it. No chance! I could go backwards with minimum effort, but not forwards.

'Slow learner?' intruded Flint. The music had thankfully clicked off.

'Get lost. Insensitive sod.' I responded, irritated by his intrusion.

'Dear dear. Did you wake up on the wrong side of your life this morning?'

'Flint, you're being very unfair.' interrupted Pink curtly.

'She's going to be facing far worse than that as her story continues and...'

'That's not the point, we're here to help our clients not to depress them.'

'Yeah yeah.' Flint yawned. 'Anyway our dear Helena is going back to Plenni to meet Brian. Although he's dull, his problem is quite interesting..,'

'Flint. Please go. NOW. Helena can meet Brian for herself and Panel specify that interference is simply not permitted!' said Pink, her voice did not increase in volume when she was annoyed, her words were just pronounced more clearly and firmly.

'Nag nag nag. I am merely Brian's elected stand-in as his nominated guide has not arrived yet. This 'problem' only ever occurs when someone behaves in a ridiculous manner, like number 16, ha. What a woman, a pyromaniac – selected Joan of Arc!! How delightfully ironic!' sneered Flint.

'Did you get her, Joan of Arc?' I asked.

'Absolutely not that would have stretched Panel's resources beyond the limit.'

'I hope that you're proud of yourself Flint.' chipped in Pink. 'That was very wrong and...'

'Au revoir, my dear Helena.' said Flint as he clicked off.

'Such a difficult man, so frustrating and unable to follow the schedule. Quite infuriating!' she added.

'Yes, but interesting Pink, you must admit he is both incorrigible and appealing, what a mixture.'

'Yes well as you picked him so you're bound to say that.' she added huffily.

'I wouldn't be able to cope without you Pink, truly.' I meant it, Pink played by the rules and at least tried to introduce things gradually.

'Thank you Helena.' she paused. 'Now we must move on. I think that you now understand the full power of the blocker. You must be patient, everything will become clearer as you progress. You need to focus on today. As Flint has already told you of the new group member Brian, I think it only fair to warn you that he may be a short term visitor, a 'hopper' as we call them. Mental health issues are taken very seriously and we can't afford to take any risks.'

'Haven't we all got mental health issues Pink?' I asked.

'Addictions and obsessions are all serious, but it is the degree of harm that has to be considered.'

'But surely taking any 'normal' person back to revisit the worst moments of their lives and relive them is a risk?' I asked becoming annoyed.

'Some people can cope and move forward far more easily than others and we're not here to cause any permanent damage, quite the reverse.'

'Does a Hopper simply return to their own life, just return drop back into their previous existence?' I asked becoming excited, maybe I could be returned to my life.

'Pink, I am surprised by your naivety. This woman has an obsessively questioning mind. She will persist. Helena you must focus on the here and now. Your questioning technique is sophisticated, but it will do you no good. You must learn patience my dear. There is no ultimate ending, no absolute closure. What happens later is irrelevant and will be shaped by what you do now!' Flint chipped in, uninvited as usual.

Following that speech both Pink and Flint signed off and I found myself rather speedily thrust into Plenni.

I was sat in my usual seat, back in the old jeans and T-shirt. There were no special lights and costumes tonight. Non-descript music played softly in the background. The emptiness made me shudder. I'd spent enough time alone and introspection was too draining. I slapped on a plaster and crunched on a Victory V. There was a fizzing sound and a flash and thankfully the arrival of Shauna.

She smiled at me and reached for her goodies instantly. I noticed that she looked a little jaded.

'Are you alright Shauna?' I asked.

'Fuckin' 'ell 'elena! That last session was a bleedin' nightmare.' she paused and looked down. I saw myself spaced out. Watched myself getting' high then descending into a downer, then loosin' it. It was just awful, fuckin' awful.' Shauna put her head in her hands and began shaking her head and moaning. I sat back, waiting for the moment to pass. Sometimes you just needed your own space. After a few moments she raised her head, took some blues and started to rally round.

'How you doin' kiddah?' she asked gently and then continued.

'Great Plenni that last one, I'll give it to Barry, he knew how to go out in style. New bloke tonight poor bleeder, it's shite when you first get here.'

I nodded knowingly.

'It's not so good when you've been here a while.' I added. She nudged my elbow and smiled.

'Anyways up, where's Andy? Too busy fantasising about bloody sheep!' she laughed to herself, jumping when Andy suddenly materialised.

'I might be Welsh but I'm not deaf Shauna!' Andy said quite pertly.

'Anyhow, good evenin', how are we?' he asked grasping for his plasters whilst casting a cursory glance at Brian's stash.

'Don't even think about it.' responded Shauna, who never missed a trick.

'Where's the new bloke then?' asked Andy. 'No point dwelling on Barry's departure whether it's up or down or wherever the hell you go from here. We need to balance up the testosterone...'

He was interrupted by a flickering of lights and the air crackled and spat with electricity. With that Brian made his entrance. He looked somewhat startled on his arrival and who could blame him.

'What the bloody hell will happen next!' he exclaimed as he attempted to take in his surroundings. We introduced ourselves and the goodies as he nervously slapped on a patch and eyed the blue tablets cautiously. Andy didn't miss a trick.

'If you don't want them boyo, I can swap you for these silvers.' said Andy in an almost pleading tone. Brian looked over at him, winked and swallowed all three.

'What the hell.' he said and smiled. He had a nice smile enhanced by a row of pearly white teeth. He looked about 40. His light brown was cut very short, but threads of grey were still just noticeable. If he had an accent I couldn't detect it, but he spoke with great energy and enthusiasm, his brown eyes alive with curiosity.

We explained a little of the very little that we knew. He asked the inevitable questions and seemed eager to join in. Shauna seemed quite taken with him.

'So er Brian what was yer job like, before you came to this shithole?' she asked tentatively.

'Social worker, the youth age range.' he replied.

'Oh shit!' she responded. 'Bleedin social workers, I 'ate 'em.' Her new found attraction melted instantly away. Brian covered a smile with his hand.

'Shauna we're not in Plenni to like each others jobs, just to help each other get through this as best we can.' I protested, perhaps a little too strongly.

'She's a right rat bag.' added Andy.

'Ah well. We'll see. Wait til he starts askin' 'open ended questions' and paraphrasing your comments so you can find 'inner meaning.' and don't forget the fake smile and concern!'

Brian laughed, a jolly heart felt laugh. 'Very good! I like it. In fact I like you.' He said quite openly and smiled across at Shauna.

'Ah fuck off.' she said quite gently and smiled to herself. The atmosphere improved.

'Oh by the way Brian, who have you chosen as your guides?' I asked.

'I'll tell you mine when you tell me yours!' he said with a grin. 'It's only fair as I'm last in.'

We told him one by one and enlightened him about Barry. His laugh was infectious and the mood became playful. As he began to explain his choice I noticed that he had started to line up the dishes and place them at right angles. He noticed me notice and for the first time he looked uncomfortable.

'We all have something Brian, that's why we're here.' I said quietly and looked away. He sighed and moved the dishes to one side and then told us.

'Cilla Black and Bruce Willis. They're my guides.' He stated proudly.

There was a moment of silence, only a moment. Shauna started first. She began with just a slow gurgle and then could contain herself no longer as she burst out laughing as did we all. Brian looked a little stunned, but soon recovered. Through my laughter I asked him why.

'Bruce was always the good guy, an action hero to help me escape and Cilla, well Cilla she has a kind of compassion with a scouse kick.

'Imagine their kids!' blurted out Shauna.

'You'll have to get Alan to meet up with his old buddy Helena. And Mel Gibson and Anneka can have cocktails with Cilla!'

'And Dame Judi.' I added.

Brian began to join in with the laughter.

'They could put on a musical like *Grease* with Bruce as Danny and Cilla as Sandy. I can just see them singing *Summer Nights*.

Andy was really enjoying himself now. It was great that everyone laughed.

'Welcome to Plenni Brian and havin' the piss taken out of you!' said Shauna. We all nodded and did a group high five as the lights flickered and back we all went again.

Big Spender
Shirley Bassey

'Wake up sleepy head!' Flint's voice cut into a very confused dream. I made a mental note about the music which he had selected for me, as tactless as ever.

'Thanks for the musical reminder, as if I needed one.' I muttered.

'You're welcome dear Helena. Now pay attention. I don't have the time or the interest, quite frankly, to repeat this. Pink is tied up with some self harming crisis, waste of time as far as I'm concerned which is why they probably sent her.'

'Definitely.' I agreed.

'Thank you Helena.'

'You're welcome.' I said and began stretching to try and force myself awake. 'OK Flint, knock yourself out. But please explain the next slice of torture properly, in a way that I can understand.' I said.

'Aren't we the little controller this morning.' Flint sighed. 'Ah, time is precious when there are so many other morons to brief, so I'll cut to the chase. Ready?'

'Yes, oh heartless one, do your worst.'

'Delightful.' he paused. 'You've moved house, yet again. You are now living 'back up North' with the inimitable Jamie. You have purchased a brand new house, Jamie has a good job, and your parents are supporting you as always. Your daughters are both well and thankfully too young to have any conception of the cock ups you both make.'

'Thanks.' I responded. I could feel the old cold empty feeling in my stomach returning and shuddered in an effort to make it go away.

'It won't do you any good to shudder.' he stated, reminding me again that he could tap into my inner thoughts.

'Just fight off the nausea and face it! ... You can do it.' he added as an afterthought. 'Anyway we discussed it at panel and thought it would be a good idea if you watched yourself at your first Gambler's Anonymous meeting.' he said quite slowly, annunciating each word in a typical Rickman manner.

'I went for two years!!' I shouted. 'Two sodding years. Why on earth would I need to relive that God awful experience!!'

'Because my dear, we think you do. And, more to the point, you have no choice!' he was clearly agitated.

'Great! Thanks a bunch.' I sighed. This was a place I really didn't want to revisit.

'Seriously Helena.' he said calmly. 'You may remember the meetings, but you haven't watched yourself from the outside. You may be pleasantly surprised. Learn something about the way you coped.' again he paused before reverting to his usual abrupt self.

'I must leave now and reassure another of our pathetic guests using my winning guile and empathy.' he said sardonically.

I couldn't help smiling as I imagined his wicked expression.

'And before you ask, yes you do have to. It's not been dealt with and you can't continue without a re-visit. Ah yes, one last thing the session begins with a quick reminder of why you started going in the first place. Ciao.' and with that he was gone and I clenched my fists as if preparing myself for battle.

The screen crackled and I was sat opposite my youthful self in the lounge of the new house. I looked at my tortured, lean face and recognised the stressful position I was sat in, as I puffed on another cigarette blowing the smoke towards an open window. The girls were asleep in bed and the small clock on the mantelpiece chimed two o'clock. It was another of those endless nights where I had waited up for Jamie. It was just plain horrible watching myself, helpless to comfort or reassure. The bruised eyes stared dejectedly into oblivion. What a complete bastard Jamie was! Anger rose within me burning like hot lava. How could any decent human being do this? The waiting, the not knowing and the ultimate sickening dread of the inevitable confrontation. God how I regretted the time and effort I had wasted on such a selfish swine. I was just reaching my pique of fury when I saw a change pass over the younger me. My face suddenly blanched, even my lips seemed pale as I felt the familiar surge of panic racing through my body. I simply watched my younger self take the stairs two at a time, but didn't need to follow. I remembered. I knew where and what I was in search of. I thought I heard the gasp after the zip of my handbag was torn back, I felt the stab of betrayal. Why did I even think that Jamie could have a genuine excuse, what was wrong with me. I stared at my broken young face as the contents of the handbag were strewn over the floor. I watched myself examine and re-examine the mutilated cheque book. The cheques had slyly been taken from the back of the cheque book to avoid discovery for as long as possible. What a coward! I thought to myself.

I seemed to have gone into some sort of state of shock and had to watch myself hugging my stomach and rocking gently. I knew why I was devastated, Jamie had promised and cried and begged for yet one more second chance. The house was mortgaged up to the hilt, he had lost his job several times, a combination of Thatcher's merciless politics and sheer tomfoolery on Jamie's part. He had on occasion 'forgotten' the time, place and clients he was meant to be working with. Impossible to live with and a nightmare to cope with on a daily basis. The responsibility of raising children at such a young age had finally tipped Jamie over the edge, I could see it now, but would never have accepted it then. As the sobbing began, I needed to go back. I'd had enough.

'Yes, yes. Alright. No need to over react!' Flint butted in. I was so relieved I could leave. 'I'm afraid that I can't take you back yet. You see a decision was made at Panel and...'

'A decision made about my life and me watching it like some sort of distorted reality TV programme, a decision about me viewing *my* life is AGAIN dictated by others!!! I don't think so!! I don't WANT to see any more of this shit today! Don't think I don't remember, I do!! I just don't need to re-live it!!!' I was shouting,

I knew I was shouting. Then came the soothing voice of Pink.

'Helena you need to calm yourself. Flint go and torture a small animal somewhere, it's more fitting for your nature.' There was a click and I knew Flint had gone.

'Look we don't have much time. Let me put it to you this way. The wound is open, it would be better to make a clean cut and heal, than to keep jabbing at it and re-opening it. We are looking for some sense of closure. You will only have to revisit this revisit after Plenni if you don't do it now. And you will begin dreading it and that will ruin the fun and release of Plenni.'

I had calmed down.

'I know, I know! By the way that was a good analogy Pink, the wound thing. I'll do it if it's just a snapshot, not the whole meeting. I don't want or need to remember the entire thing.'

'Consider it done, we'll make it brief and put you straight into the Gammanon room.' This was where the 'victims' or innocent partners went whilst the Gamblers started the steps of recovery.

'Thank you Pink.' I said meekly.

The screen crackled and sure enough there I was sat in my old place, next to the gurgling tea urn in a small L shaped kitchen. This was the Gammanon meeting held in a social club in central Manchester. Gammanon offers advice and support for those on the receiving end of the addiction. Seven other souls were jammed around a square table covered with a floral, vinyl table cloth which was commonly to be seen at children's parties. I glanced at myself, thin, drawn, and weary, but determined to make my life work out and my family stay together. The Serenity Prayer was chanted and I could hear it being murmured in the next room, where the people responsible for our collective demise were having their own meeting.

God grant me the serenity
To accept the things I cannot change:
Courage to change the things I can:
And the wisdom to know the difference

The kitchen was reserved for the innocent only. I was shocked again as I heard some of the tales of violence, alcoholism, abuse and neglect that were told in the sanctuary of that kitchen. I watched my face and knew what was going through my young head. In the Serenity Prayer we ask God to help us to accept the things we cannot change. Jamie may be able to ask, Helena had asked long ago, when the Rottweiler wielding debt collectors with their sovereign gold rings banged threateningly upon her door. Jamie may be able to accept what he couldn't change, but suddenly Helena realised she couldn't, not now and not then. My past self suddenly looked up and there was a flicker in my eye, I watched as my head seemed to turn and acknowledge my future self.

'Oh MY GOD!! PINK I can see me! I mean she or me can see me!! Get me out.!!'

'Flint Code 10 ! Emergency !!' I heard Pink's voice.
   My eyesight began to flicker and stars appear, similar to those in the aura you get with migraine.

'She's transposing!! We mustn't let them combine!!' shouted Pink

I felt myself drifting, weightless; I was floating above my youthful self. Suddenly my old self looked up and grinned. This was like *Back to the Future*, but with more sinister overtones. I was terrified.

'Gotcha!' was the last thing I heard from Flint. Everything crackled and fizzed and then it all went black.

Against All Odds
Phil Collins

'She is perfectly alright Pink!' Flint's strong tone of voice cut across the music.

'I think this song is particularly tactless.' Pink added.

'Helena likes it.' Flint said defensively. 'It makes her smile.'

'I am here you know!' I added, not yet having the courage to open my eyes. 'I think the line, 'Take a look at me now, there's just an empty space' is rather appropriate.' I added, referring to the song, which then went off immediately. 'It's OK Flint, I don't mind and it does make me smile Pink.'

'Huff.' muttered Pink. 'Anyway Helena we're both here today as we have a grave concern about your welfare. Do you happen to remember what happened at the re-visit?' she asked cautiously.

'Of course she remembers!' shouted Flint. 'Don't pussyfoot around the girl. She's awake and all is well. Is that not right Helena?' he asked.

'I do have one question for you all knowing ones.' I paused.

'Aha!' said Flint.

'What the hell happened to me? Old me smiled at this me, almost wickedly. As if she could see me!! Is this some mad, horror, sci-fi special which I'm acting in? Maybe I've crossed the line like some possessed method actor and I've starting living my part… like Dustin Hoffman or…'

'Desist!' interrupted Flint. 'Nothing that wildly romantic or intriguing. A slight glitch on the system. You are correct on one score though, your past self did, at the time, seem to be aware of your presence and unusually was not taken by surprise.'

'You mean it's happened before? Tell me, come on what happened!'

'I think that Helena has heard quite enough for now. Yesterday was quite a shock for her and she had a lot to face up to.' said Pink quietly but firmly.

'Blah blah blah, I'm not a child Pink. Flint I demand you tell me!! What happens if my past and present meet? Does it defy physics, blow the machine, cause a mind meld…'

'Good God woman! You're a maniac. Pink, you deal with this movie crazed client. I have bigger fish to fry. Emergency beeper. Tootle pip my dear.' and with that there was a click and Flint had gone.

'Come on Pink, tell me something, surely I deserve that.' I paused.

'It scared me to be quite honest. Have I been back before? Is that it?' I asked.

There was a pause and a beeping sound.

'Listen Helena, it's complicated. It is time for Plenni which I feel you need. You are not in any danger and I need to consult with Panel before I continue. I can assure you that we will discuss the incident with you, but my hands are tied at present. I would ask that you are diplomatic at Plenni, Brian is having a tough time and this may unbalance him.' she added.

'Unbalance **him**!!' I almost screamed. 'It scares the shit out of me!!'

'That's enough. I have said what I can. Now, would you like to meet your friends? There is nothing more I can add at present.'

'Fine.' I paused. 'I would like to go to Plenni, please.' I didn't want to miss seeing everyone and knew that Pink was not able to throw any more light on the incident.

'Good. Here we go then.'

There was the usual clicking and crackling of static and back we all were at the familiar table all dressed in our casual jeans and T-shirts.

'Where've you bin?' asked Shauna. She had a wild look in her eye.

'What's wrong?' I looked around the table.

'Take yer gear.' she thrust the goodies at me. I felt uncomfortable. I duly slapped on the patches and crunched my victory V, leaving the blues until last. I looked over to Andy, Brian seemed anxious to retie his shoe lace keeping his head well down.

'What's going on?' I asked addressing Andy directly.

'How was your last re-visit?' asked Andy. 'Both guides present and correct?'

Shauna looked directly at me. Brian gradually surfaced from beneath the table.

'Anything unusual?' he asked, his eyes widening.

'Don't beat around the fuckin' bush. Summats up. One of my guides has done a runner.' announced Shauna.

'Not Anneka Rice? I can't believe it! I know she can run fairly fast but she didn't seem the type.' I exclaimed.

I caught sight of Brian smiling as he began picking his finger nails. He looked nervous, jumpy and who could blame him.

'No you daft cow! Not the lovely Annie. Richard, Richard Branson. Bastard's disappeared with that bitch from *Countdown*!' she almost shouted.

Andy smirked, Brian whimpered and I forced my lips into a crinkled smile and managed a frown at the same time.

'Who the hell's got Carol Vorderman as a guide?' I asked.

'Some stupid cock from C block. I met 'im once. He was a hopper like...' she stalled and looked down.

'Like me. That's what you mean isn't it?' Brian asked directly.

'Yeah, if you have to know, like you. Causes loads of problems, coz the guides get switched and...'

'Shauna, you can't tell me that it's anything to do with Brian or being a hopper that's lead to Mr Virgin Branson coupling up with Carol detox maths genius! Anyway where does that leave you now?' I asked.

'I'm not bloody sayin', totally ruined my street cred.' she said looking crestfallen.

'Don't be such a misery guts Shauna. Come on my girl can't be that bad can it?' chipped in Andy.

'We'd love to know. Well I would anyway.' added Brian.

'Me too! Come on tell us who the lovely Anneka is partnered up with!' I said enthusiastically. We all looked at Shauna expectantly.

'You got someone off relief list, that's it I'll bet.' said Andy. Shauna looked down.

'What's relief list?' asked Brian looking at me.

'No idea Brian, I've not been here that long either.'
I said.

'It's the fuckin' no hopers list, like celebs from *Big Brother's house* that no bugger knows or likes.' she said quietly. 'And you only get to choose from two of them.'

'Ah like a stand in. that sort of thing?' asked Brian carefully.

'Yeah, that sort of fuckin' thing.' she said, obviously irritated.

'Come on my love.' said Andy 'Can't be that bad, look at Brian's choices. I mean Bruce Willis fair do's but Cilla Black!' We all smiled.

'No offence matey.' added Andy, who winked at Brian.

'No problem.' said Brian slapping on a plaster.

'It's garbage. I got no fuckin' say you understand.'

'Of course. It could happen to any of us. Randy old Branson hey. Best keep you eye on Mel lovely eyes Gibson Andy, he could be next, better not make a play for Dame Judi.'

Shauna smirked and let out a tiny laugh. Brian began to giggle which started Andy and I off.

'Imagine their love child?' said Brian. We all laughed, even Shauna.

'You'd better keep an eye on your precious Rickman, Helena. You're not the only client on his books, he's a bit of a client tart.'

'Leave Alan be!' I responded.

'Oooh.' they all said in chorus.

'Anyway, I'm intrigued now. Come on Shauna before we all get blasted back into the nightmare of our own lives. Tell us, we won't judge you.'

Everyone turned to look at Shauna. She blushed slightly.

'Fuck it, might as well say. Remember he was not my bleedin' choice.'

'We know!' we all said together. Shauna muttered something under her breath.

'Sorry what was that?' I asked.

'Keith Chegwin.' she said sombrely.

I looked at Andy who was biting on his lip as Shauna glared at him. Brian looked back down at his laces and then disappeared under the table in a fit of giggles. I was the worst. After such a challenging session beforehand, I seemed to lose self control and let rip.

'Anneka Rice and Keith Chegwin! Fan bloody tastic!!' I laughed aloud.

Brian surfaced from his pretend lace tying still giggling and smacked his head on the table letting out a huge guffaw. Andy held his sides, laughing loudly. We all looked at Shauna. Tears were streaming down my face.

'At least we can't see our guides Shauna.' added Brian. 'A naked Cheggars would be enough to put anyone off!' Shauna smiled, then shuddered as she visualised her guides naked. Her face broke into a smile.

'Fuck it, you guys, glad you're having a laugh at my expense.'

'Just think you can play *Cheggars plays pop* together, Branson doesn't know what he's missing!' said Brian.

'It was him or Des O'Connor.' added Shauna in a dead pan voice.' That was enough to start us all off again. Even Shauna started to laugh. We all linked arms and enjoyed our moment of hilarity as the crackling started and back we all went.

Money Money Money
Abba

'Rise and shine Helena. Another wondrous session awaits you, my dear!' enthused Flint. 'I hear through the Panel grape vine that my name was mentioned amongst you reprobates at Plenni yesterday. Fame has its price, as I know only too well, you only have to look at what I'm doing now!' he added somewhat cynically.

I yawned and struggled to shrug myself awake, not feeling too enthusiastic about another session.

'That's as maybe Helena.' Flint rudely cut into my thoughts. 'But it's better not to forget why you are here.'

'And to think I defended you.' I said with mock remorse.

'I am always pleased that I'm *not* mentioned.' Pink cut in.

'Jealousy is a sin Pink, especially when it is so thinly disguised.' clipped Flint.

'Anyway they said you were a 'client tart" I added. I could hear the faint, infectious giggle from Pink in the background.

'How divine! One of my better compliments, if I say so myself. Not very imaginative, but flattering in a base way.' he said thoughtfully.

'How terribly loyal of you to defend Mr Rickman, although I fear he is beyond any reasonable defence. Alas, we must move along. Have you briefed her Flint, or is that a ridiculous assumption. Could we possibly turn the music off? Yet another tactless choice.'

'Any chance of a day off? Don't you guys get a day off or don't they have them here beyond the Thunderdome?' I asked.

'Sometimes you're just plain stupid.' said Flint. 'It's not a holiday camp, there is no remission for good behaviour, we are trying to sort your life out! Anyway you'll have plenty of days off if you don't get this right!'

'Enough Flint, you can't blame the girl for asking.' said Pink kindly.

'Too soft woman, which I might add came across in your sympathetic portrayal of Queen Victoria, *Mrs Brown* wasn't it?' he sneered.

'I believe you showed your feminine side in *Truly Madly Deeply* if I'm not mistaken.' she retorted curtly.

'Balderdash! That was just damn fine acting.' he responded somewhat quickly.

'Children, children settle down. You're both my heroes. That's why I chose you.' I said attempting to sooth bruised egos.

'Unfortunately, I must depart from this intellectual debacle; I have been beeped yet again and must guide yet another bewildered member of my flock through his compulsive nightmare of a world. Adieu.' and with that he clicked off.

Pink sighed. 'He can be rather trying at times.'

'Trying I may be, but deaf I am most certainly not!' Flint chipped in.

Pink sighed again. 'Well without further ado or inter-ruption we must move along. Prepare yourself Helena I have only time for the briefest of introductions. You are on holiday in Wales with your parents and your two girls. Jamie has dropped you off and is meant to return for a few days and then transport you all home.'

I groaned. 'Not this one. I can remember it perfectly well Pink!'

'That may well be the case, I don't choose the sessions, and there must be a good reason behind this selection. There were an awful lot of events Helena. I will admit that you have not had the easiest of times.' she said quietly. 'Prepare yourself.'

I closed my eyes against the crackles and flashes, holding onto the fact that at least I would see my daughters again.

I opened my eyes. I was stood in a room with bunk beds and smiled as I watched my two girls aged about 3 and 5 opening their back packs and chattering away to each other excitedly. Both girls were dressed in cotton summer dresses and strappy pink sandals, I desperately wanted to hug them, stroke their hair and feel their little bodies next to mine. To reassure them and help them get through this awful period of our lives.

I gasped, as I saw my much younger self enter the room. I looked thin and worn, weary of life. My face was lean and you could see the bones beneath my cream t-shirt. I was feigning excitement and responding to the bombardment of questions about the beach and the sea. Explaining carefully how daddy had had to leave and go back to work, a shadow crossing over my tired face already aware of the uncertainty I felt about his departure. I followed everyone down into the lounge where my young looking parents were waiting. Sammy ran into the room and jumped immediately onto her Papa's knee and began her incessant questioning. Ellen toddled over to her grandma, arms out waiting to be picked up. Once on her grandma's knee she nestled her head under her chin and began playing with her beads. It was lovely to see everyone together, knowing that through it all real families stick together. The screen flickered and the scene changed.

I was stood outside a phone box, watching my former self making a call.

I could see my fear and anxiety so plainly through the thick glass panes, hear the tension in my voice, I knew what this call meant. I was speaking to my lodger, a young student Georgie, who was telling me that Jamie had not been home until the early hours. Georgie occupied the fourth bedroom, we needed the cash and she needed a decent place to stay while on placement. She must have wondered what the hell was going on. I was asking about the post, about green envelopes from the bank and she was telling me that one had arrived. I knew then. I watched the horror cross my face, the late night twinned with the inevitable arrival of a credit card added up to only one thing. I could hear myself thanking the unknowing student for her help and watched as my younger self replaced the receiver and slid down the wall of the phone box and began hugging my knees, tears of total despair slid down my face. What a complete and utter bastard!! There was no coming back from this, I knew it then as I do now.

I turned away as the heartbreaking sobs raged. This had been my life, years of my life. The screen crackled and we moved on.

Now I was in a Church. I had forgotten all about the little Church across the road from the cottage until now. I looked at myself sat in a pew. Never a very religious person, but heartbroken and hoping for answers. I had forgotten about this place and my frequent visits whilst on this 'holiday'. I looked broken. I watched my lips mouthing words I couldn't hear, but knew. 'Why. Why. Not again. It's enough.' This was my mantra, my cry for help. The consequences of this would be massive. We would lose the house, each other. I knew then and now that Jamie would have lost his job again and that would have been enough of a trigger to start the roulette wheel turning, draining us of any future life. This was painful, unbearable, I was powerless to move closer or walk away. Thankfully the screen crackled.

In the next scene I was kissing my girls after their bedtime story, reassuring them that spiders don't always fall on the top bunk of bunk beds and even if they did they don't have teeth and can't bite. Distracting them from the endless questions about daddy coming back. Mum and dad had been fantastic, as always, doing the beach and the sandcastles, ice creams and fish suppers. Making it a real holiday for their grandchildren, as they would do many times more in the future. These children deserved better. I watched myself go down the stairs, beyond tired. Mum and dad knew that he wouldn't be coming to collect us. Numerous phone calls and information from the lodger clearly outlined the nature of events. I looked at my tired, thin frame and wondered why I had put up with this garbage. He was a complete waste of time. I knew that then, but still believed that people got married for ever and men should be there for their children. *What God has put together, let no man pun asunder.* I just hadn't worked out that in my case we would all have been better off without him. No-one's a 100% bad. And when your children adore their dad and look like him and have fun with him, it's hard to break the ties that bonded you together. At this stage of my life I knew that I still wanted things to be sorted out and get back to how they had been. I could see it in myself then, the resignation to my lot, the ways that I enable him to behave as he did, my dogged determination to make this tattered marriage work. What a waste of my time, my life....

I watched as my mum and dad worked out yet another plan to get us all home. He had deserted us, again and this would not be the last time. This was just the beginning, I knew that and facing this crap was draining as he lied through his teeth yet again. A compulsive gambler is just what it says on the tin, no-one can do anything to change that except the person themselves.

A solution was found and my parents rescued us again from what should have been a lovely family holiday. They never reproached me, interfered or criticised until things got far worse than this, which they inevitably did. I took one last look at my dead eyes and slumped body and called for Pink to get me out of there. I'd had enough. To live it once was hard, twice was too much for anyone.

'I understand.' I said, to anyone who could hear me. 'Get me out of here PLEASE!' The screen crackled and flickered.

I could hear Pink's voice very faintly.

'It's alright Helena, just relax now. Try to breathe slowly. In and out, in and out.' she said slowly.

Then there was the familiar smell of menthol, reminded me of hospitals, I was drifting, falling backwards and then nothing.

Don't look back in anger
Oasis

'Stop prevaricating woman and put the girl on snooze. We should do it now, before she comes round!' said Flint somewhat testily.

'I think that's unfair Flint, I always like to give my clients the option. It's the very least we can do when they are forced to face such emotionally disturbing memories. Helena needs Plenni and the interaction of others, a concept you may find difficult to comprehend.' snapped Pink, obviously agitated.

'This isn't a bloody Human Rights convention Pink! We have a responsibility for her mental welfare, as her guides. Helena quite simply lost the plot, we don't use the menthol blocker for no reason.' he stated loudly.

I could, of course hear this verbal sparring, but as yet was unable to respond. My head felt light and I was drifting in a menthol haze.

'She will **not** thank you for that Flint! Having to go straight into another session when she comes around will be much more damaging. And it is a rather special Plenni tonight, with the guest hopper putting in an appearance.' she added determinedly.

'Are you suggesting that Helena will suffer in some way if she misses the psychic drivel offered by

Miss Bernadette the incredible clairvoyant?' he asked sarcastically.

Suddenly, I felt more alert and quite frankly, quite interested. I didn't want to miss out on this opportunity!

'My dear Flint,' I said gently. 'Thank you for your concern, but I think it would be more beneficial for me to go to Plenni. I'm feeling much better now.' I added.

'Huh! Anyway you're meant to be sleeping.' he added gruffly. 'Guides are called that for a reason.'

'Well, thank you for your advice, but I'm awake now and would like to go to Plenni.' I said steadfastly.

'I'm so glad you are feeling better Helena. We had to use the menthol blocker to bring you out, I'm afraid your vital signs were showing distress. We are not here to traumatise you.' said Pink.

'And that is why you should go onto snooze and sleep it off!' Flint said raising his voice slightly.

'I don't want to go straight into another session Flint. I have slept soundly and need to move on!' I was adamant that I was not going to miss meeting Shauna and the gang and of course the mysterious clairvoyant.

'I agree.' stated Pink resolutely.

'It is of course, your choice.' said Flint, clearly annoyed and with that he clicked off.

'Oh dear, I didn't mean to …'

'That is so typical.' interrupted Pink. 'Shall we move on to Plenni now Helena, time is marching on. You know now that you have a guest and may have to prepare your friends for her arrival. It's been quite a chaotic time and we are short of guides.'

'That's fine Pink. Get me out of here please.'

There was the usual clicking and fizzing and flashing of lights and then I was there in my seat facing a rather troubled looking Brian.

It took me a few moments to adjust to my surroundings, it felt great to be away from the room and the monitor.

'Hi.' said Brian somewhat wearily. His brown eyes looked tired and bloodshot.

'Hi, are you OK?' I asked. 'Where is everyone tonight?'

'Ten minute time delay or something.' he paused. 'I'm glad really. I just wanted to talk to you.'

'OK no problem. Not sure I'll be any use to you. I've not been here that long myself.' I said, feeling secretly pleased that he wanted to speak to me.

Brian looked distressed. 'I hate it here.' he said shaking his head. 'The sessions are a bleeding nightmare. I have no control over where I'm sent or what I see.' He looked straight at me. 'I had to watch the beginning of my illness – I remember of course, but I didn't need to be put through it again. How do you cope? What's it all for?' he put his head in his hands. 'When will it stop?' He seemed desperate, I understood.

'I know exactly how you feel. We're all in the same boat. They just had to knock me out with some menthol anaesthetic thing because I wasn't coping. We have no control, you're right and it's really tough.' I said feeling angry.

'But is it real? I mean do we just wake up in our own beds if we make it?'

'I'm sorry Brian I just don't know. I do know that Andy knew he was going somewhere, we had a party. He didn't know where he was going, but just before he went, he told me to work it out. And the guides, I think that they know things, but you have to be careful. They're in our heads and…'

I was interrupted by the usual flickering and white static. I looked over to Brian and winked. 'It'll be OK, talk to me again.' And with that Shauna and Barry arrived together.

'What's up with you two misery guts?' asked Shauna.

'Anybody would think someone had died!' said Andy smiling and we all smiled.

'Brian was just asking you know, the usual questions that we all ask when we first get here.' I flashed a warning glance over to Brian and I could tell that he understood to keep quiet about our conversation. After all Shauna wasn't exactly discreet and Andy had his own problems.

'You'll be alright with us Bri,' said Shauna. 'Learn to use Plenni as an escape from those bleedin' mind mashers or you'll go fuckin' mental!' She was right and we all nodded.

'I 'eard a rumour.' stated Andy. 'Don't know if it's true like, what with all the buzzin' in my head.'

'Spill the bleedin' beans Andy. It's not as if we get much soddin' excitement around here.' Shauna said.

'Well, here it is, we might be getting a visitor.' he paused and I nodded. 'You 'eard it too H?' he asked. I nodded and signalled him to tell the others.

'Anyhow it's like this. Our visitor to Plenni. It's a clairvoyant,'

'Who the fuck is she then?' asked Shauna.

'Well I dunno.' said Andy.

'You know her name though.' Shauna said and Andy looked confused, we all exchanged glances.

'Just that she's clairvoyant, that's all I know.'

'Big deal. She's runnin a bit bleedin' late this Claire whats her face.' Shauna said seriously.

I looked at Brian who grinned and then at Andy who was biting his lip.

'Shauna…' I said, but she interrupted me, picking up on the atmosphere.

'What's the big fuckin' joke? You already met this Claire or summat?'

We were all laughing. Brian slid down in his chair trying to disguise his mirth. Andy had his hand over his mouth and I had a fit of the giggles. Shauna was getting increasingly annoyed. Andy was the first to recover and respond to Shauna.

'Her name's not Claire Voyant, she is a clairvoyant.' he said carefully.

By this time it had dawned on us that Shauna had no idea what a clairvoyant was. We were into dangerous territory as Shauna's eyes began to flash with anger. Brian stepped in.

'I can see what you're thinking Shauna.' he said kindly. 'It's just a stupid name for someone who is psychic, in touch with the spirits that type of thing.'

'What a load of bloody garbage!! I want nothing to do with that shite!' said Shauna angrily.

'You don't have to do anything you don't want to do Shauna.' I reassured her. 'None of us know what to expect.'

The lights in the room flickered and the static crackled. Bernadette was about to materialise. It was quite a slow process and reminded us all of our precarious existence. We all seemed apprehensive.

Bernadette looked as scared as we felt. A woman, probably in her late fifties with a grey bob, dark eyes and a pretty face. She looked around the room and at each of us in turn.

'I'm Bernadette.' she said, pronouncing her name with care. 'It's my first visit to Plenni, I only arrived in this world or existence or whatever it is, last week. I think if I understand it correctly we are between worlds, which is quite honestly no surprise to me, yet it is quite terrifying in practice.' she smiled nervously. Shauna turned her head away in anger, still smarting from her earlier mistake. We all introduced ourselves in turn and I kicked Shauna gently to prompt her to join in.

'I'm Shauna. And you can keep yer fuckin voodoo powers well away from me. I had enough of that mystic plane shite when I was trippin' out on heroin.'

Bernadette didn't look phased. 'I see.' she said calmly and then adopted a more business-like approach. 'There is a lot of trauma in this room, I can sense the fear.'

'I could've told you that for nowt!' said Shauna shirtily.

'I have no idea how long I will be here for or how long I can stay.' She said.

'None of us do Bernadette.' I said slowly. 'Erm do you know anything that could help us, I mean what's your gut instinct?' I asked.

'At this early stage it's very hard to say. The voices are confused; after all it's been a very disturbing journey moving into the light.'

That was a mistake, I thought to myself.

'Moving into the light! It's not bleedin *Poltergeist*!!' said Shauna and we couldn't help laughing which relieved the tension. Even Bernadette smiled.

'You're a very strong character aren't you Shauna?' she turned and stared at Shauna a very long, hard stare. Shauna flinched. Bernadette looked over at Brian. 'Toby wants you to know it wasn't your fault.' she said quietly. Brian went white.

'What!' he said.

'You know what I mean, sorry I had to say it.'

'Yeh well don't say anything else or I'll twat you one.' said Shauna fiercely. I heard the very faint beeping of an alarm and realised that we could be shut down, remembering what Flint had said previously. I had to move in.

'Come on guys let's try and guess who Bernadette has chosen for her guides.' I said desperate to change the mood. Andy picked up the gauntlet aware of how much we needed to end on a positive note.

'Russell Grant and Ann Diamond.' Andy guessed first.

'Actually you couldn't be more wrong.' said Bernadette.

'Jeremy Paxman and Mystic Meg.' Brian blurted out.

'Bet I fuckin' know.' said Shauna joining in.

'Doris Stokes and John Noakes, him off Blue Peter!'

Even Bernadette was laughing now.

The lights flickered and we knew we hadn't got long.

'Tell us, tell us, we all begged.'

'None of you were even close.' she stated. Her brown eyes flickered merrily. Although Shauna was the closest. Shauna gave us all a smug look.

'Brad Pitt and Valerie Singleton.'

We all exchanged glances and then Shauna began to giggle. We all joined in and gave each other five, even Bernadette. All was well in our surreal world. The air fizzed and back we all went.

Blinded by the light
Manfred Mann

Nice one Flint, I thought to myself as the music blared loudly and I began waking up, smiling at his rather too relevant choice of music. It served as a valuable reminder that the Panel listened in to Plenni. Perhaps due to boredom and of course our exciting repartee.

'Don't flatter yourself.' interrupted Flint. 'With the carnivalesque cluster of celebrities inhabiting the Guide's world, we don't fall short of excitement, just intelligent conversation. I mean it isn't everyday that you encounter Brad Pitt arm wrestling with Keith Chegwin. Not to mention the bizarre experience of encountering Mel Gibson and Victoria Wood playing country music together. Nauseating. Pink loves it, of course, all that sense of community and fair play.'

'I see, so you're just the miserable bastard then.' I said.

'He is indeed.' said Pink quite firmly. 'Not really a team player are you my dear Sheriff?'

'Alas, we must move on from the mundane to the sublime, I refer of course to Helena's life.' he said dryly, not one to take criticism too well - I thought.

'Pink, give her the low down would you, I'm off to give some other pitiful moron the benefit of my wisdom.' and with that he was gone.

'How are you feeling this morning Helena?' asked Pink gently. 'Did you make the right decision in going to Plenni?'

'Definitely.' I said. 'We had an interesting time. We met Bernadette, the clairvoyant.'

'Ah. I feel that it would be prudent to keep an open mind and a safe distance from someone who may or may not have a message for you. I've never been totally convinced by that sort of thing.' she said carefully.

'Pink, we are sat God knows where, doing God knows what! You can hear my thoughts and we have no idea what will happen!! We could all be dead or merely on a stop off along the way to Death Valley! And you're worried about a message I may or may not get!!' There was a long pause.

'Right. Well then, moving along.' said Pink curtly.

'I wasn't getting at you Pink. Honestly, it's just the weirdness sometimes overtakes me. You understand.'

'Actually I do.' said Pink. 'We all feel it at times, but there are magical moments, when things come together, when there's a good result, it's simply fantastic!' said Pink with a slight tremor in her voice. I had to play this one carefully.

'Is a good result when someone goes back Pink, goes back to their own life or just gets released from this in-between world?' I asked, vaguely aware of the faint sound of an alarm.

'Helena I can't say. I am a fool for even mentioning it, it's not fair to any of us.' she said sharply. I could tell that the subject was closed and knew that there was absolutely no point in trying to get any answers.

'Now Helena we're going back to the first disappearance, you know what that is so I don't need to explain. Just watch yourself and try to be more objective. We don't want you to have the trauma of another blocker.'

It's about six weeks after the holiday incident. This session has been selected because your memory of the way you react, will have become diluted by the extensive number of traumatic incidents that punctuate your life. Your raw response to this first incident should give you an insight into the learned behaviour you exhibit in stressful situations even now. I think I've got that right. Anyway that's the idea. Are you ready?'

The dragging feeling had started again in the pit of my stomach. Flash, bang wallop and off we go again!!

I was back in the family home, on the landing watching my weary, younger self sat on the floor of Ellen's bedroom reading a story. The girls were freshly bathed and giggling together in their pink pyjamas with their glossy, clean hair. I could almost smell the Johnson's shampoo and baby talc. Ellen listened intently, her round eyes like saucers as she lay back on her *Care bears'* pillow. Sammy wriggled around, asking a multitude of probing questions whilst trying to juggle with her magic teddy. Ellen began snuggling down and her eyelids began to droop like wilting flowers, a sure sign she was ready to sleep. I gently closed the book and watched the familiar movement as I swing Sammy onto my shoulders, kissed Ellen and gently clicked off the light. I followed my former self into Sammy's room and smiled, even at this tender age it so typically represented her character. Books about animals were scattered over the floor, accompanied by discarded drinks and odd socks. In the corner there was a creative display of soft toys, no dolls of course. Sammy was about 5 years old and very definitely had always been a daddy's girl. She was a perceptive child, highly strung and able to pick up on things quickly. Unfortunately, she had heard and seen things she shouldn't have in the traumatic turmoil which pervaded in this house. Ellen was too young, thank God; she was just 3 and blissfully unaware of the domestic unrest.

'I'm not going to sleep anyway.' announced Sammy quite definitely. I watched my painfully thin body sigh as I set up the tape player and moved some of the debris off the floor. Sammy had never been a good sleeper, as a baby she'd been a screamer and leant very strongly towards the hyperactive.

'You can't make me.' she added, in a matter of fact tone which I remembered very well. Her green eyes set in a determined glare which defied defeat. The night time battle was very familiar and a regular occurrence. I knew that Ellen would already be fast asleep. I watched myself following the bedtime routine to the letter – the teddy, the tape, the kiss, the discussion and then it began. Sammy sitting upright on top her *My Little Pony* quilt cover and refusing to lie down. More kisses and reassurance and then there was only one option, almost simultaneously my past and present self left the room. There was no point in switching the light off. All three of us knew that this was not the end, this was only the beginning of bedtime. I watched myself walk unconvinced down the stairs and could see Sammy up and about rearranging her soft toy zoo ready for her next sortie.

There had been no *Super Nanny* programmes or extensive behaviour guides, no parenting classes beyond babyhood in the mid eighties. Naughty corners and methods of anger management were not on the cards – you just did your best. At this time some authority was still exercised by the father and at this time most fathers didn't leave after conception. Clearly it was only a matter of time for me, but my young innocent head refused to entertain the idea, strong family bonds and a sense of what should be, drove me forward.

I caught up with myself in the kitchen, blowing smoke up through the kitchen window, biting my lip and wondering yet again where the hell he was. I was absent mindedly putting cutlery away into drawers. My essays for my degree course lay untouched on the table once again. The phone rang at 9 o'clock and we both knew it would be my mum, anxious to check on the the ongoing saga.

The screen flickered and moved me on into the lounge, four hours later. The scattered books and toys signified the many more entrances from the sleepless Sammy. The house was quiet now and the carriage clock showed the time as 1.10am. I noticed that the ashtray had now been transported into the lounge and the small window was open, as were the curtains. I took a good look at myself. My hair was patchy, skin blanched, black rings circled my eyes, my thin body strained. The double quilt wrapped around me in an attempt to stop the shaking and a sign that I knew it could be an all night session.

I had dragged the phone into the lounge, it never rang and was too late to call anyone for support. This is a very lonely time and apparently when most people die and having spent numerous nights sitting alone and waiting in the silence, I can understand why. I saw myself start at the sound of an engine, which turned out only to be a late night emergency at the neighbouring ambulance station. The sirens were not allowed on until they got to the main road. I had been in this situation many times and looked sympathetically across at myself, realising that there would be much much more to come.

Everything flickered and the time was now 4.30.am. I was watching the back of myself as I knelt on the floor phoning the local police station. I could almost hear the Officer's words,

'Sorry madam, you can't register a person missing until at least 24 hours have passed. You see it could be that your husband has broken down or something's erm cropped up, late night....'

I knew that Jamie wasn't coming back that night. I could feel the anxiety prickling and was beyond tears both then and now. I sighed dreading the oncoming school run, the long drive to Uni and yet another essay I hadn't done. What a bastard!! We were trapped in debt, claiming benefit, with a meagre student loan to use for food. It felt hopeless, desperate and I was definitely very alone.

The screen flickered. We were both sat in front of a policeman. I was giving details and descriptions in a very shaky voice.

'It's more common than you think love.' stated the policeman, trying to sound reassuring. Little did I know how 'common' this would become.

'He'll turn up. They usually do. The serious stuff we get to know about and we've checked the hospitals.'

He was kind, trying his best, but obviously aware of what people who go missing can do. It was the not knowing that killed you, the waiting and worrying that wore you down. This episode continued for 4 nights and cost us thousands of pounds in gambling debts. Sammy had been distressed and unable to understand, as we all were, where her daddy had gone. I knew then that this was just the beginning of a much bigger game on the playing field of our marriage and it be a struggle to survive. I'd forgotten the sheer fear and absolute pain of being deserted and rejected and the heavy weight of responsibility which eroded you daily. I turned away from the scene and looked at the maternal photograph which I still have, my mum and me and my girls. I closed my eyes to move myself away from this. Everything clicked and flickered and I knew that they taken me back, everything went black and I was grateful they had withdrawn me and closed me down.

I ain't missin' You
John Waite

'Some people are just plain cruel. Flint, would you please switch that dreadful music off!' whispered Pink.

'Never fear Pink, I gave her enough Drowser to knock out an elephant. I don't think she'll make Plenni. It's so difficult to judge the exact amount especially when there's pressure on, I didn't see you rush for the medical tray Pink.'

'No that's quite true.' Pink paused. 'Poor Helena, she's right in the thick of it now. I've grown quite fond of her and those little girls, did you look down and see them last night Flint, simply adorable.'

'It may surprise you Pink, but last night I was trying to stop Number 8 from carving his name in his arm with a hypodermic he'd 'borrowed' and then had to administer oxygen to Helena's druggy friend as she started hyperventilating and as the other loser, what's his name... the OCD fellow...'

'Brian,' added Pink

'Yes Brian, he's in the next pod and heard the sirens and pressed the emergency alarm. I went in to thank him once the crisis was over, of course and found he'd disconnected himself from his support machinery and was trying to prize the door open with a metal strip that he ripped off the breathing machine. He's quite desperate to leave here. I think that he's a dangerous friend for our dear Helena especially in this vulnerable stage of her journey, I would have thought that...'

'I didn't know they'd paid you to think Flint!!' I almost shouted. 'It sounds more like blatant interference and nosiness to me. I'll choose my own friends, if you don't mind, even in this plastic surreal twilight world, whether I'm already dead or in limbo – I WOULD like to make my own choices. So BUTT out and keep out of Plenni or I will go to Panel!! Even weird nightmares have ways of escape or redress and...'

'Yes yes, very noble I'm sure. The buzzer went for Plenni whilst you were delivering your Freedom of Rights Bill. Would you like to go or continue babbling onto deaf ears and by the way, you don't have any 'rights' here, you ARE extremely lucky to be here. Don't forget that DEAR Helena and what the alternative to being here is!' he said in a menacing tone.

'You don't scare me Flint! And I don't really believe ...'

'Helena, I can only apologise for Flint's somewhat brusque approach, but I don't want you to miss out on Plenni.'

'Brusque approach, that's very mild!! He's just bloody rude and so insensitive, God alone knows why I picked him...'

'Charming! I can block you going to Plenni Helena, should I choose to.' he paused. 'I won't because that would be damned cruel. Be careful with your comments my dear, I will turn a blind ear to them this once.

Mark my warning well, your future may depend upon it.' and with that Flint clicked off.

'There's no more to be said on the matter Helena, I think it would be for the best if we just sent you to Plenni.'

The familiar clicks and flashes and crackles and I was gone.

I was the last one of the established group to arrive this time and arrived into the middle of what appeared to be a very heated argument. Thankfully Bernadette the psychic had not yet arrived.

Andy was desperately trying to calm Shauna and Brian down.

'It'll do you no good. I dunno a lot myself, but I do know that if you rock the boat they remove you and I'm sure you don't go back to your life.' stated Andy.

'Who fuckin cares!! You might as well be dead as putting yourself through this painful shite!!' Shauna said heatedly.

'I agree with Shauna. I think we're suffering physically not just mentally.' said Brian.

'Anyone here want to go through my withdrawal for me? I collapsed yesterday and that's nothing. I DON'T WANT to watch myself go through that. At least when I was going through it, I didn't really know I was going through it and that's the best way!! I don't want to watch myself going through ECT (Electric shock therapy) I was sedated, why should I want to see the rerun in full Technicolor?'

'I understand all that and maybe you could ask panel for some sort of Fast Forward type deal. But listen to me, you can't escape it. We don't even know if it's real anyway.' said Andy.

'I know what you mean.' I agreed. 'But they seem to have the power and we are in a very vulnerable position which …'

A sudden crackle and bump and Bernadette arrived.

'Hey Shauna, Claire's here.' joked Andy. Bernadette grinned unconvincingly.

'Morning, afternoon or evening.' she said uncertainly. 'I'm in need of some answers.'

Bernadette looked tired, anxious.

'Are you OK?' I asked remembering how terrified I had been when I first arrived.

'We're all in the same state today Bernadette. Shauna doesn't want to face her rehab re run, Brian tried to escape from his pod with a piece of metal,' a ripple of admiration went around the group and Brian smiled proudly. 'I definitely don't want to see the police interrogation I've got coming and Andy, well actually Andy how are you doing?' I asked. 'You've been here the longest.'

Everyone looked over at Andy.

'OK here's what we do. First let's all take our goodies – we're never here for long so move it.' The group nodded in agreement and slapped on our silver plasters and administer our various tablets. A feeling of well-being seemed to flow through the group.

'Brian did you see anything through the door?' he asked tentatively.

'No, but I did managed to disconnect from the bed. I think I got about 5 minutes before they zapped me and the alarm went off.'

'Right. You got further than anyone else has. I decided to try and question Branson whilst we were chattin' about business. You know how direct he can be. I wanted to try and find out the timescale, how long I'm stayin' where the bloody 'ell I'm going.' he paused. 'I don't think I've got long here. Anneka kept interruptin'. I think they know...'

'I know they do, well at least mine do.' interrupted Bernadette.

'Why have you read their fuckin' auras or done a mind meld.' asked Shauna cynically.

'Nothing that impressive.' responded Bernadette. 'I think they got their transmissions crossed and I was privy to a conversation between Val, Valerie Singleton that is and Mel Gibson.'

'Hey Hands off!! Mel's my fuckin' guide.' reacted Shauna.

'Shauna calm down. Bernadette might be onto something here. Remember we're all in this together! Carry on.' I said gently.

'Well Mel was saying that he was quite busy and liked a challenge and Val said she thought that her client, which is of course me, wouldn't be a long termer like hers. So Shauna looks pretty certain to stay for some time. I do have the label of 'hopper' so I knew that I would be here on a temporary basis. My feeling is that there is a master plan and for most of you, you have the time to work through your issues. Perhaps we could all start carefully questioning our guides.' she was speaking very quietly. 'And Brian I meant what I said about Toby. I don't seem to have my usual contacts and messages coming through here – but that one was persistent.'

'He died.' blurted out Brian. 'A child in my care, a tough case - I missed the signs. I started with the OCD after he hanged himself.'

'It's only a thought. I'm not sure if I should say this.' Bernadette hesitated. 'I think he may be trying to help you Brian. If you like I'll try and contact him before next Plenni.'

Brian looked desperately sad. 'I don't know...'

'Don't be a fuckin whimp.' said Shauna tactlessly. 'If Mystic Meg here can help us out with this psychic bollocks then give it a try!! Our lives are on the line here! Or our deaths!!' she added.

Brian nodded slowly. OK Bernadette do your worst.'

'Right oh then, here's how it is.' said Andy with an air of authority. 'Everyone ply the most sympathetic of your guides for any scraps of info. Bernie you do whatever it is you do and try and get a message from this Toby. Helena you need to avoid any direct run ins with Rickman, there was a rumour before you came that he had been pretty merciless with one of his clients. Shauna you work on Mel, he knows more and I'll go for Branson. Are we together?'

We all put are hands on top of each others on the table and gripped on tightly.

'Remember they can get into our heads and our thoughts.' I added. 'I've found a way which works for me. I just think of a brick wall...'

'Like in that fuckin film!!' enthused Shauna.

'Yes Shauna just like in that fuckin' film. Get your scraps of info and conceal them behind you own wall or whatever works for you.'

'I have a secret hiding place in my mind and lock those secret thoughts away.' said Brian.

'OK it's all getting a bit bleedin' weird but can we all do it?' said Shauna enthusiastically.

'Yay!' we all cheered and had our first group hug for a long time.

'May the force be with you.' said Shauna. 'And let's make sure we're goin' to live long and fuckin' prosper!!'

Everyone laughed and relief swept through the room before the clicking began. We all nodded our heads and braced ourselves and as the lights flickered, our first team plan was born.

With a little help from my friends
Joe Cocker

I heard the music before I opened my eyes. Damn Flint, he was far too intrusive and perceptive. Not that Pink wasn't, but somehow she seemed to be on my side, kinder, gentle…

'I'm not.' interrupted Pink. 'At least I'm not if Flint is around. Remember that Helena, he is better connected than I am and more influential. Be careful please…' Pink went quiet. I realised for the first time that I could be endangering her and fell silent.

'I will say this and then speak no more about it. Flint is busy with a violent vomiter down on D block. He'll be in a foul mood if and when he gets here. You are right to fear him Helena and your Plenni group should fear him also. He has a history that I cannot discuss, but mark my words and tread very carefully to protect not just your remaining lives, but those of others. That is all.'

Silence choked the room. I felt flattened, suddenly aware that my actions and those of my friends could have dire consequences. I gritted my teeth as a familiar feeling began in the pit of my stomach. Oh no!! Not this!! I was withdrawing as I used to, shaking, beginning to close down.

'There are choices to be made here.' burst in Flint as the music clicked off. 'Pink, you're gently, gently approach has served its purpose. Kindly leave.' ordered Flint.

'I leave when Helena asks me to leave Flint, you'll find it in subsection 3 of the ruling on Client Care.' said Pink curtly.

'Namby pamby, lily livered bunch of softies!' stormed Flint.

'Actually Pink, I would like to go to my next session now if you please. Thanks for the offer of a tete a tete Flint, a while ago I would have been very grateful – but now I feel that I have to sort out my own shit – so how about just letting me get on with it.' I said determinedly.

'How delicately put Helena.' Pink said with a slightly smug undertone in her voice. I could imagine her smiling her closed lip, twinkly eyed smile. I felt myself laughing on the inside as I was catapulted back into my past. For once I was glad to go – gruelling as it was, at least there were no surprises there for me. Just re-runs and mini sequels which were sealed, set, living memories playing themselves out until - well until I could leave them behind to fade and fragment into the background.

A sharp crackle and blinding white light deposited me into my old kitchen. (this process seemed to have become significantly quicker each time – a made a mental note to bring this up at the next Plenni) The younger me had the obligatory cigarette and the radio blaring away, some stupid misplaced love songs – a form of escape, I suppose. The girls were watching TV in the front room – I could hear the childish singing and the odd thud of a cushion as I knew they would be dancing on the chairs and then diving off them into a commando roll. I turned and looked at myself. The patchy hair and drawn face I could take, but the shadowed eyes and beaten stare shocked me. Naturally I had lost weight in those nightmarish times, my bones were angular and obvious, but in my memory I never thought of myself as beaten. Emotionally battered and disheartened– yes. Financially screwed by remortgaging to pay off gambling debts and frequent periods of unemployment – agreed. But I felt that I'd always been a fighter, maybe that had been on the inside and I'd never really paid any attention to what it was doing to me on the outside. I remember the feeling of being trapped, powerless to change or undo the mess that had been thrust upon and me. Unable to rewind, go back and change direction. Was this my lesson? To learn to let go and move forward?

Instinctively, I knew that the doorbell would ring and braced myself. My old and new self seemed to inwardly cringe and the stomach cramps came back. I watched my young self act quickly. The cigarette thrown in the sink, kitchen window shut and back door locked. I then followed myself into the front room, sat both girls on the same chair away from the window and switched the volume on the *Rug Rats* cartoon right down. It had always struck me as strange that Sammy – now aged about 6 always seemed to understand when something serious was happening. I few nights earlier we had had a charming visit from one of Jamie's 'employers' who had wanted money back for a job that Jamie had not done. A ridiculous job - which he could never have done. Jamie had lost the money and done another disappearing act leaving me and the girls on the front line – yet again! Sammy had pushed Ellen into the Wendy house which we had up in the corner of the lounge. As Ellen was only 4 she responded well to Sammy's unusual enthusiasm for singing one nursery rhyme after another. I had always known that she was aware of things and in moments like these always protected Ellen despite the usual sibling rivalry.

I watched myself close all the doors into the hall which isolated the front door. A shaking hand slid the safety chain across. It had always been difficult to get a clear view of any visitors, as a small rectangular piece of fish eye glass had been set into the door, just at eye level. This distorted faces into demonised, beak like beings, which normally proved to be more frightening than the visitor themselves. In this case it wasn't. There is nothing more sickening than this particular type of 'visitor' to your home. Even the police or play group leaders organising the rota! I remembered that this particular charmer had already been around once that week. The door opened about 6 inches and I positioned myself in such a way that I could see his face clearly this time around.

The man must have been early thirties, with a grubbily shaved head and a creased neck, where the waves of fat lap right up to the edge of the old hair line. The black leather jacket and black trousers, both neat but shabby, accompanied by black shoes with a hint of a shine but not convincingly leather. The man was giving his mock friendly smile and unconvincing, sympathetic eye crease, as if he gave a shit. His dumpy, sovereign ringed fingers, rubbing together impatiently, taking the occasional break to twist the rough metal studs in each ear. Obnoxious, grubby little bastard! Who would do this job? It must be difficult to sleep at night!! This was the first time I had been given the opportunity or had the where with all to study this insincere little worm, one of many of our 'visitors' who don the mercenary title of bailiff. In my limited experience, the 'debt collector' how lovely, is often from the very background he/she seems to betray. The people they 'call on' are not wealthy, fat cats or high flyers with massive bonuses – these are people used by banks and finance houses to reclaim money from the desperate and the damned – at that time, I belonged to both. It was not a coincidence that these people visit at tea time, before it goes dark – just to ensure that they are seen 'visiting' or taking goods from your house. The ultimate humiliation for anyone, especially when houses are built so close together. A real treat for the neighbours. I interrupted my observation for a moment to check my progress. The arrogant little git was semi – smiling as I tried to explain that I hadn't had the money, that the gambling slips were not in my name and that I didn't have any money to give in settlement or part payment.

'We don't care if you've had it or not luv. It's a joint account. We can't get him so we have to come to you. Banks and credit card companies just hand your debts over to us. Simple as.'

'That's so unfair!' I protested. 'I don't even know where he is. I have the kids to bring up and we're on benefit.'

The man looked squarely into both our eyes. Hard, relentless. He turned only once to silence the two rottweilers which were barking in his car. It was terrifying.

'I can't, no let me say won't, leave empty handed.' he said menacingly. Both the young and old me seemed to take in a sharp intake of breath, I immediately knew that I had to check to see if the downstairs bathroom window was locked. I hurtled down the hallway and sighed with relief. My younger self seemed to pause before turning to face the man.

'I don't have anything to give, he sold anything of any value, you know that...' my voice cracked and the shakiness grew more intense.

'Is that a TV I can hear?' he asked cockily.

'Yes. But that's all we have left. Jamie sold the video weeks ago.'

'Look, you're just wasting my bleedin time!' he raised his voice and I wanted to smash his head with the door. 'Give me some cash or I'll take the TV. Simple as.' He locked into a threatening stare.

I watched my old self going into the kitchen and reaching to the back of a cupboard to get the old sage jar down. This was the pot that Jamie had not yet found and money that was given by my parents and sister for 'emergencies' and school trips was hidden under the herbs. I watched myself hand over the scented ten pound notes through the gap in the door.

'There that wasn't too hard was it darlin'?' he smiled, one of those half grins.

'It'll do for know. Be back Thursday for the rest. Oh and if you're out I think it's time I called on your neighbours, show my concern. Am sure on an estate like this they'd be itching to know about the nocturnal habits of Jamie. Word of warning now, if he turns up again get the cheque book and cards off him. The bank won't let you take your name off the account until it's clear, but at least you can stop it getting any worse.'

And with that I shut the door and walked into the lounge. Two shiny haired little girls bounced onto my knee and hugged me, uncharacteristically quietly. I had never explained much at this stage and only in later years had I tiptoed through the land mines of our past, determined that they should not be affected by this nightmare situation.

From a distance it seemed even more sordid - how could Jamie have cared so little and left us with all that! My older self came out of the lounge, unable to watch as I knew how many years I would have to contend with threatening visits, loan company phone calls and police visits. I sighed. Enough. A flash, crackle and pop and I was back in my pod. Not medicated or plunged into unconsciousness, just quietly drifting, my mind racing, but I was coping, facing it and surviving.

Money's too tight to mention
Simply Red

Good old Flint, I thought to myself, never let's me down. I was feeling curiously OK, that low ache of dread in my stomach which I had been waking up with had eased. I was just stretching myself out and yawning when the music suddenly clicked off and the screen in front of me started flashing an ultra violet blue. Then came the siren, piercing, it seemed to be screeching in desperation. Pink's voice cut over the siren,

'Helena, don't panic. I'll be with you as soon as I can. Stay calm my dear...'

'Pink! What's happening? Please tell me. It sounds serious!'

'There's been a breach and...' she lowered her voice, 'and I think it's someone from your Plenni. I have to go now Helena.' Pink clicked off.

The lights dimmed. Helena lay in her pod wondering who had set off the alarm. Her gut instinct told her that it was Brian, he'd seemed the most unstable at Plenni and if he'd been taken back to the point when Toby had taken his own life, it may have sent him over the edge. Then again, Bernadette was an unknown quantity. Maybe she'd tripped the alarm by straying too far or had one of her attempts at contacting Toby have tipped the balance. Not forgetting Andy of course, he was after all coming to the end of his time. Would he have been more prepared to take risks now that his time was nearly up? What if he couldn't hack it any more and had breached security?

The alarm stopped suddenly and the screen in front of Helena returned to a static white fizz. The lighting returned to normal.

'My my, quite the little detective aren't we?' interrupted Flint. 'I can see your reasoning Helena, would you care to make a decision, not one of your best qualities I know.' She heeded Andy's warning, not to rile him especially under the circumstances.

'Well, – I er, think it may have been Brian, just because he's new and quite unsettled and because he did already manage to free himself from his bed.'

'I can see that you may have been swayed by his escape attempt with a strip of metal.' added Flint in one his caustic tones of voice. 'But you need to be very careful Helena, your Plenni group are meddling – only to be expected – but the guidelines are clear and binding. Never forget that your presence here is a chance, a chance for your and your fellow inmates to redeem yourselves, a chance that not many people get.' Flint was uncharacteristically reflective.

'Flint. The incident has been resolved.' cut in Pink.

'Will one of you tell me now?' I asked carefully. 'Please, before we go to Plenni?'

'It was Brian.' Flint stated bluntly. 'He attempted to cross-wire some of the equipment, a primitive attempt which would never have worked of course. He has had the final warning from Panel Helena, make sure that he doesn't take this lightly or you'll have one less team player at Plenni. You should all be focusing on your own issues, God knows you have enough, instead of planning The Great Escape.'

'Don't misread the opportunity that you've been given Helena, the place that you were all originally heading for doesn't have a 'get out clause' or a 'get out of jail free card' – don't waste it by focusing on the whys and wherefores.' said Pink slowly.

'Your time here is limited. That goes for all of you. Brian has the most to lose and he is the newest member. There is nothing that your group can do that hasn't been tried more efficiently and effectively. Stop wasting our time and yours, before this chance is taken from you.' and with that Flint and Pink both clicked off and I was thrust into Plenni in a matter of seconds.

Andy was already there, talking somewhat heatedly to Shauna.

'Ah Helena thank God! What do you know? My guides didn't come to me before I came to Plenni and Shauna was just told me that it was 'probably' Brian!'

I shared the scraps of information I had and stressed the seriousness of Flint's warning and the veiled threats over each group members' future here. Bernie had arrived as I was speaking and nodded her head in agreement.

'I was given exactly the same story. Brad was quite excited by the whole affair, Valerie more concerned. She gave me a stern lecture in her *Blue Peter* voice. I feel sure that Brian is still with us, but his distress levels are dangerously high.' she added, joining us all as we slapped on our patched and crunched our Victory V's.

'He's very late and we need to support him. Sod the plans for now, we're on very thin ice here. This is our lives or whatever you'd like to call it that we're gambling with...'

The familiar flicker and crackle announced Brian's arrival.

Brian was extremely pale and shaky.

'You alright matey?' Andy asked cautiously. Brian looked down at the floor.

'Fuck it!' said Shauna. 'Come on, I don't normally do these pussy Oprah moments, but if ever a bleedin' group hug was needed its now.' and with that she moved over to Brian. 'Get off your arses you miserable buggers!' and without further ado we all responded and had our first group hug that had been instigated by Shauna. Brian relaxed into the mass of bodies and the contact was appreciated by all. We reluctantly returned to our respective seats.

'Right now you daft bastard, what the bloody hell have you been doin'?' asked Shauna.

'What do you know already?' he asked cautiously. I explained the extent of our knowledge. Brian nodded. 'I've had a warning from Panel and I think Plenni is being heavily monitored or censored. What I can tell you is that they were sending me back to a meeting with Toby and quite honestly I was scared shitless!' Brian looked around at the group his brown eyes brimming with tears. 'I just didn't want to go, it was like a nightmare for me to have to watch that scene again!'

'What did you do then?' prompted Andy gently.

'I tried to cross-wire the circuits first, but I got a massive electric shock which must have triggered the alarms. Last time they tried to send me back, I tried imposing a mental block, but they bypassed it. They shouldn't be able to make you go back, not if you simply can't face it...'

'Rickman told me straight that we're on dangerous ground. He said this was a chance we've been given and that the alternative, well I think the alternative is death.'

'But you don't fuckin' know that for sure H do you?' asked Shauna getting heated.

'We none of us know for sure.' added Andy. 'Could be a nightmare, a hallucination, an out of body experience on the operating table.'

'Maybe we could all try and remember where we were and what we were doing before we arrived here.' I said.

'Barry and I tried that one my love.' said Andy. 'They put a blocker on. Remember how they did with your kids Helena?'

'Shit, yes, that's that out then. 'I looked over at Bernadette who was frowning and looked deep in thought.

'Bernie, what are you thinking?' I asked as I passed Brian his goodies, which he immediately used.

Bernadette shook herself into the present. 'I can only go off my instinct here and the messages they sometimes send me...'

'Who's they?' interrupted Shauna.

'I don't always know that.' she said simply.

'Go ahead Bernie, we're lost in the dark here. Just share anything, we don't have anything to go on.' I added.

'She's right.' encouraged Andy. 'No matter how stupid or insignificant it sounds. We need help here lovely.' Even Shauna nodded reluctantly. Brian simply reached out his hands to hold and everyone in our circle held hands, for comfort rather than any supernatural reason.

'Well. I think we were all facing death at the point in our lives when we came here. Either through emotional or physical means. I think that our lives are on hold, held in some sort of stasis while we sort out these issues.' her dark eyes glinted as she attempted to work through her thoughts. 'We have power in our strength as a group. Brian has already managed to ruffle the feathers of the system, Andy has experience as he's been here a while and seen people come and go, Helena is developing her blocking device, Shauna is resilient and has quite a presence and I, well I can sometimes hear or see things that we can use.' she paused. 'I want everyone to put any prejudice and preconceived ideas to one side. Focus on the silver plaster that is on the dish in the middle of the table.'

I heard Shauna sigh next to me.

'Give it a chance Shauna.' I said quietly. She shrugged her shoulders.

'Nothin' to fuckin lose I suppose.'

We all stared hard at the silver plaster. The lights flickered, just for a moment and the silver plaster flipped over.

'Jesus Jones!!' exclaimed Shauna snatching her hand away.

'Team work, I think Bernie's right!' said Andy excitedly.

'I'm not into this spooky crap, but If it gets us out of this shit hole well...'

'We need to be careful, block this memory, everyone, NOW quickly before they take us back!' ordered Andy. 'We all obeyed.'

Brian seemed more cheerful, glad of the contact. We all knew that time was short.

'Hey Bri, don't rewire the circuits and leave us all stranded in our pasts!' joked Shauna.

'Worse than that don't cross wire me into Bernie's bleedin flashbacks or I'll feel like I'm Whoopi Goldberg in that film *Ghost*.'

'I don't think Patrick Swayze could deal with you, young Shauna.'

Everyone laughed.

'Wouldn't have minded a bloody turn with him in *Dirty Dancin*!' she added.

'I think it would have been more of a blue movie with some very 'dirty' dancing!' said Andy.

Shauna started humming *I've had the time of my life* substituting the word *life* to *death*. Andy started to giggle and then we all started as the lights flickered and back we all went.

That's what friends are for
Dionne Warwick

F or the very first time the sound of the music didn't wake me. I hadn't slept or been drugged by a zapper or switched off or whatever it is they'd had to do to me. My mind had been working overtime. New ideas and the excitement of us all pulling together had made my mind buzz and ideas were still fizzing in my head. It was a complicated procedure trying to tease out and pull through a new idea, which once coaxed into the foreground, had to be protected by the blocker to prevent Flint and his cohorts from getting a snifter. The more complex and imaginative ones were the hardest to confine, slippery as eels, they twisted and slithered, reforming and reshaping, then darting in different directions and refusing to be pinned down.

'I didn't realise that you were partial to our slippery friends, especially at this time of the morning.' Flint interrupted. 'I hear from our dear Pink, that we didn't have to pull you from one of your tawdry episodes and that sedation was not required on your return after your last session. This is a marked improvement. I think that you will need to brace yourself for the next one.' he paused. 'Unpleasant, but necessary.'

'Yes, but there's no need to traumatise the girl before she's even set off, is there Flint?'

'Nag nag nag. It's better to be aware of these things in advance...'

'That's in your world, we're not in the Airport in *Die Hard* now.'

I could hear Flint chuckling to himself.

'You really know my films quite well, don't you Pink?' he said somewhat flattered.

'Well... yes,' she paused. 'I suppose I do. I'm quite fond of Bruce in that particular film.' she added.

'I see. Charming.' and then he continued with his unmistakable ice crystal cutting tone. 'I always felt my performance in 'that particular film' was outstanding, compelling, even inspirational – anyone can play a bare footed, gun slinging over rated cop with a dysfunctional life and a sickly relationship with the 'black police officer' on the outside. I brought clarity and a cold calculating presence to my roll...'

'Well that's as maybe, but Bruce has softness about him, a vulnerability – it's appealing and...'

'Appealing to the unfairer sex. Ah ha! I know how Helena felt about my performance in *Truly Madly Deeply*. I feel that I can push the buttons of the female audience when I choose to.'

'Anyway, we all have our own preferences, I'm sure you have yours...' muttered Pink.

'You should ask Helena.' stated Pink quite plainly.

'Why? I'm not trying to prove a point or reinforce my masculinity...'

'I am here you know.' I interrupted eventually.

'Well?' asked Flint.

'Well.' I paused, my turn at last, to have the edge over Flint.

'Get on with it.' he chipped at me.

'Well, yes there was something, you were rather, well to be honest rather you.' I realised the implications of what I had said after I'd said it, as usual.

'I think Helena just paid you a compliment.' said Pink cautiously.

Flint coughed.

'Typical women always going off at a tangent– never focused on the job in hand.' and with that he clicked off. Pink chuckled, that deliciously infectious chuckle and I wished I could see her face and twinkly eyes that lit up mischievously when she laughed. I allowed myself a quick chortle.

'That was lovely Helena, what a refreshing change. Such a pity to have to send you back again.' she paused and composed herself.

'You're much stronger now.' she added. 'Are you ready Helena, let's get the next one over with.'

'OK.' I said firmly, time to face more demons, but somehow it felt different and I felt more in control and less of a victim.

The familiar fizz, crackle and flash of bright light sent me straight back to the old family home. I walked into the lounge, drawn by the sound of laughter and looked upon an almost idyllic family scene which brought a tear to my eye. The monopoly board was laid out on the floor and a game was in full flow, for once with us all playing. It was strange seeing Jamie, myself and the girls all together. I watched transfixed, smiling as the little girls tried to follow the game.

They were clearly delighted at playing even though they were really far too young. It was interesting that my past self allowed the odd cheat and second chance, whilst the competitive nature of Jamie would make no allowances to his young daughters. Even so it was a typical family scene and I enjoyed each moment as I knew only too well, what was coming.

First of all the power went off. I watched myself go instinctively to the phone, but the line was dead. My stomach clenched now, and clearly then. I was able to watch Jamie carefully, as I hadn't been able to look at him at that time. He looked bemused and walked to the window as if waiting for something to happen. I saw myself sit both the girls on the settee on either side of me. This incident was one of the final blows in our turbulent relationship that would cause not only heartache, but humiliation.

The sound of cars, travelling down the Close at uncharacteristically high speed, broke the moment. Jamie blanched and the children looked startled. The reflections of flashing blue lights filled the living room. Three police cars and an unmarked car screeched to a halt in the cul-de-sac in front of our house. The aggressive pounding on the front and back doors frightened us all and Ellen began to cry. Jamie let them in and the CID Inspector produced a warrant. At this point I ran to the door and asked if I could take the children to my friend's house around the corner. The cocky, aftershave laden Inspector sneered at me. Luckily the PC who I had called for a missing person report was stood behind him and nodded me through.

'I know this lady sir, let her take the little ones; I'll go with her if you like.' The Inspector shrugged his shoulders noncommittally.

'Whatever. Jamie boy you don't move!' he ordered. I watched my past self move, but I stayed in the house. Watching the gathering crowds of nosy neighbours form clusters and gossip together, arms crossed. My heart sank, the stigma started here for me and my girls.

I watched sadly as Jamie was frog marched to the settee by the smarmy CID guy. The numerous police officers had already started rummaging through the house, clumsily ripping open drawers and rooting through personal possessions. They were avidly searching for something. I heard the door close as a very shaken young Helena returned, face drained of colour and hands shaking. We both heard the CID Inspector read Jamie his rights, head bowed and ashamed, he was arrested and forced into a police car like a common criminal. The police had cut the power and the phone line, this must be serious. Jamie was driven away and then I watched a scene that had stayed with me for a very long time.

The house was buzzing with activity as the police officers searched each room. The sickening sound of drawers being wrenched open and belongings being tossed to the ground rattled through the house. The front and back doors were still flung open providing excellent viewing opportunities for our voyeuristic neighbours. The CID man jammed me against the wall in the narrow hallway. The smell of his aftershave was overwhelming as he leered at me. His slick backed hair and neatly pressed suit, merely concealing an arrogance which was misplaced and unnecessary. It was terrifying as his questioning began and he forced me harder against the wall. Looking back, I genuinely had absolutely no idea what he was asking about. He kept banging on about Jamie's clothes smelling of petrol and his whereabouts the previous evening. I was shaking, in shock, unable to answer any of his questions. I never knew where Jamie was at the best of times. None of it made any sense. The worst part of it all was his rough, aggressive attitude as if I was part of the Manchester mafia and party to whatever had gone on.

'If you tell us where it is, we won't have to search your room.' he growled at me. From the corner of my eye I could see police officer throwing my children's' t-shirts and socks out of their small chests of drawers. I felt sick, then and now.

I was lead up to the fourth bedroom and he smiled as he confiscated two red felt pens.

'Forging receipts.' he stated, obviously delighted with his find. I then followed him and my past self into the garage. The Police were already searching my car, although I had no memory of unlocking it. Again the CID man grinned as he bagged up two petrol cans and an old watering can, sniffing them proudly.

'Arson is a very serious charge.' he said sneering. 'He could go down for a very, very long time. 'No-one was hurt though. Looks as though he tried to burn down a shed door to get his tools back from yet another botched job.'

I was stunned, even my present self unable to take in the gravity of it all.

'You can visit tonight after 8. He won't be coming home.' he added. The police were finishing up and eventually left. I stumbled to the phone to contact my parents and neighbour, too ashamed to face the throngs outside. The phone was still dead. I had the key to the house next door as I was watering their plants while they were away. I sneaked in to use the phone, leaving a note to explain that I had used it in an emergency. My parents set off urgently and my friend hurried over to comfort me. A new stage to the nightmare had begun. I watched myself as my hands shook to light a cigarette, what sheer hell Jamie had, yet again, brought to our home. Another nightmare chapter in my married life, which would continue to haunt me. I watched myself putting away the children's clothes and toys. Feeling disgusted and nauseous I threw all my underwear which had been ousted, into the washing machine.

A flash of light and crackle withdrew me abruptly. I was conscious and alert. Shaken, but coping. I knew this episode had to come and was almost ready for it. I had re-lived it and survived. I was getting stronger.

'Firestarter'
The Prodigy

F lint was humming along happily to himself, as I came around.

'Pink has somehow earned herself a 'rest day'.' he said somewhat caustically. 'So you have the pleasure of me and me alone, for now at least. Your 'little group' amuse me in their naivety and simplistic dabbling - but Helena you need to take heed, the psychic phenomenon is a dangerous weapon in the hands of an inexperienced amateur. Your under qualified, mystic meddler could cost you dear. Panel are of course aware of your shenanigans Helena and your stake could not, quite frankly be any higher. You have just about everything to lose.'

'I hear what you are saying Flint,' I hesitated, treading carefully. 'but you feed us just the tiniest snippets of information...'

'You do realise that if you were all in isolation all of the time, then you would most probably be too fearful to question anything! It is only **our** sense of morality and humanity that has allowed Plenni – a right, I might add, which can easily be revoked!' Flint snarled.

I could sense his anger and could, to a point see his argument. I changed tack.

'In my position, you can't deny that you would ask.'
Again a short silence.

'You fail to see, dear Helena, that you have no rights, no position – you have misunderstood. The dice are not merely loaded against you; you are not invited to the game. The chips were lost before you arrived here. This was your lucky break, your gamble – you were all rescued from death. This isn't a virtual reality show, a 'feel good' Disney film set or a scientific experiment. This is your chance, your last chance! There's nothing more, no secret escape, no miraculous finale – we rescued you! The horse has bolted, you're merely attempting to run from your very saviour. I may have wanted to ask the question – but the difference between us is that I understand the answer.' There was silence. Then very quietly he added, 'There is nothing more to say. Just see out your time, like Barry did, quietly and with dignity.' I was hesitant, but still I had to ask.

'Flint, please tell me - where did Barry go? Alive or dead? Heaven or hell? On earth or hidden here to be recycled...'

'Good God! Stop now, you relentless inquisitor. You're not in a re-run of *Soylent Green*! I will say no more. You must go to Plenni, whilst you're still able to. I warn you to take great care, your Plenni is top of the bill for Panel at present. And without further ado, with a flash, bang and a wallop, off to Plenni I went. Flint could be so abrupt at times, which meant that I was first to arrive.

The 1970's Muzak played insignificantly in the background, it had been a long time since we had even noticed the music. The goodies had already been laid out neatly to match our places on the table. I suddenly shivered and became anxious for some company. It was such a bizarre situation sitting here in Plenni alone– in my room I knew I was alone. There was a flicker of light and a fizzing sound and Shauna appeared behind me. The others followed one after another. None of us wasted any time and after cursory nods of the head, patting of arms and grunts of acknowledgement, everyone hurried to sit in their places and automatically took their goodies, in preparation for what was to come. There was tension in the room and I was so grateful when Andy took the lead.

'Right, let's get straight to it, we know that time is short. So first up, who knows what? Anything new from last time?'

'I just want to say that Alan has warned me we are 'top banana' as far as Panel is concerned. I'd like to begin by saying that I got absolutely nowhere in my quest to eek out any relevant information, Pink is on a break and Flint just thinks we're lucky not to be dead already. Sorry.'

'Same 'ere.' chipped in Shauna. 'Not a bloody snifter. I did practice that mind thing though and I've fuckin' sussed it...'

'Lovely, don't tell us now then.' Andy knew the dangers of sharing at present.

'They changed my schedule.' said Brian. 'It means that I can choose when I revisit the erm, the Toby scene.'

'That's real progress!' I was impressed. 'So there is some flexibility after all.'

'I've been thinkin' and as I'm the next to go, I thought I should push this point.' He dropped his voice and carefully covered his mouth so that no-one would be able to lip read. 'Later when they're bored of us, I want us to come together and try and cut the power. We know it can be done. I want to find out if this place is manned by people or some sort of computer. If we send the system down see, someone may have to come, doors may open, something might give us a clue on how to get out, all of us get out I mean.'

There was a serious silent nodding. Then Bernie spoke in a very matter of fact tone, so as not to arouse suspicion.

'I know how to get them to switch us down or keep the heat off.' She paused. Everyone looked at her eagerly. Just try and act normally as though we're having one of our normal discussions. 'I'm willing to relate my first clients' life story. He thought he was a dog in his past life, rubbish of course. Anyway he told me all about his very tedious doggy travels. I'm happy to share his first adventure in Skegness while we prepare. I don't need as much warm up and focus time as you all do, if you know what I mean, I can just babble away.'

'That's very generous of you Bernie. Thank you. I think we all need to concentrate as we will probably only get one shot at this.'

It was mutually agreed. Bernie launched into the tale of Timmy the terrier and his long and tedious journey, making it sound as dull as she could manage. Meanwhile the rest of us showed mock interest while sharpening up our thoughts and visualising the power circuits that Andy had alluded to. After a quarter of an hour Bernie looked around at each one of us as she related Timmy's hilarious visit to the vets and his latest sleeping position. She was good, very good in fact. Each one of us responded in the affirmative and Bernie slowed down her narrative. Then Andy started the countdown procedure in a deep but quiet voice, which could be heard underneath Bernie's babbling, as it was a few tones lower. He counted down very slowly from five. We all moved further forward and under the table the human circle of hands was made. I felt very apprehensive, not so much because of our experiment, but because of any consequences.

'Timmy was such a scamp, occasionally he would have a tinkle in the geranium pots of old Mr James...'

We were down to number 3.

'Mr James would shake his stick at Timmy, not realising that Timmy was really a human and a middle aged bank clerk at that...'

'2.' said Andy solemnly.

'It was a bit much though when one day Mr James took off his shoe and threw it at Timmy...'

'One.'

'Now!' said Bernie who had the final say.

Everyone focused as hard as they could. I could feel Shauna's hand gripping mine tightly. Andy looked pale and drawn. Brian half closed his eyes and I then closed mine. In for a penny, as they say.

The first thing I noticed was the sound. A kind of electric fizzing. I opened one eye. A siren went off just before the lights dipped and the room was almost in darkness. Then almost immediately, the lights flashed on extraordinarily brightly. A pop and high pitched glass explosion to my right, told me that one of the bulbs had exploded. I jumped, as did Shauna, when a door was being opened behind us. I had never even noticed a door behind us. I saw Bernie raise her eyebrows and Brian frowned, Andy gave one of his Welsh quizzical looks. Shauna and I had no choice – we had to turn around.

I black man in green overalls bounded into the room, muttering to himself.

'Bloody D wing. I told 'em. I said overload the main frame and that's what you get. You were very lucky this time. If this had happened in one of the..'

'Workman 17. Continue with your duties in silence.'

There was no mistaking the dominant tone of the gloriously moody Richard Burton.

'Plenni is now over and under review for this particular group at least. We are undecided as to whether or not you are all extremely devious and subversive, or as workman 17 pointed out, there was quite simply a power surge to a rather challenged main frame. We will decide and you will return to your pods. You need to focus on reviewing yourselves. Keep this at the forefront of your thoughts. If this *was* a warning shot across the bow, I suggest you turn this upon yourselves and take heed. A little knowledge is a dangerous thing.'

The sound clicked off. The workman whistled the Titanic theme tune, murdering the high notes. We sat in silence, our hands now released and rubbing worried foreheads. Within seconds we were all simultaneously removed back to our pods and the rest is a blur.

Blinded by the light
Manfred Mann's Earth Band

'Wake up you tiresome girl!' Rickman stated in a perfunctory tone. 'I have no idea what possessed your little group yesterday, nor do I need to know. However, you **do** need to know that everyone in that group is now under review, you have lost the rights to the next Plenni and will go into a double session of your delightful life. Fabulous. I only hope it was worth it dear Helena just for the sake of getting a light bulb to explode. Panel could of course decide to disband your little Plenni group, keep you isolated, alone. Plenni was seen as a humane option to make the experience less terrifying. You have abused this privilege and now you pay the consequences.' and with that Flint clicked off. I sighed. Oh God, two sessions of my life, no Plenni, no fun or relief...

'Yes, well you really should have thought of that before. What on earth possessed you? Really Helena, you have no idea at the severity of this behaviour. I know that you don't understand, I can see that this frustrates you, but you are on the way to destroying a very special chance that only a select few have been given. It's wasted on you and your group, wasted. I can only hope that you learn from this mistake, you have your punishment at a time when the sessions are particularly gruelling. Your friends will suffer too, I'm sorry but it's your own fault.' Pink clicked off, clearly distressed. I could almost imagine her eyes flashing in anger and her head moving jerkily as she spoke in annoyance. I suddenly felt very low and very alone - which was probably the intention. They would watch us all now of course, we would have to put our plans on hold, but time was pressing – Andy didn't have long and no-one really knew who would be next.

'Quite clearly it is your own fault. Now brace yourself – you know the drill!'

Flash, bang crackle and there I was sat beside my younger me in my old black Nissan cherry, affectionately nicknamed Bessie. This was partly due to the car's age and the struggle we had getting up hills and her speciality at stalling at roundabouts. Still, she did have a sun roof, cassette player and four doors not bad for the mid 1980's on a very tight budget. I didn't need to look out of the window, I knew exactly where we were going and what would happen. I looked across at myself – concentrating and singing along to *The Christians* in a mindless, rather tuneless fashion.

This part came after Jamie's arrest, at least I didn't have to re-visit that awful night when I went to the Police station. Small mercies. No wonder I looked stressed, my hair thin and complexion marked by this stressful period in my life. It was a 20 mile journey to and from Uni and I was and still am a reluctant driver at best, I never loved it. I recognised a steely eyed determination in my young self which I'd never really seen from the outside. Nothing was going to stop me getting my degree, I had decided that I would get it despite everything not because of everything. My erratic home life and battered marriage provided more than enough material to fill the pages on my Creative Writing course. English Literature was just the best subject – especially 19th Century Literature. I couldn't believe how fortunate I had been to get on the course and to get a grant.

I sensed the tension levels soaring in the car and heard the indicator and breaks being applied rather abruptly. The car seemed to fill with the sound of two hearts pounding and for a split second young Helena's eyes narrowed and she turned to look straight at me.

Good God! It's a wonder I'm sane. That was terrifying – utterly and purely terrifying. To have yourself look straight back at you – a moment of absolute truth and with such depth of knowing! It chilled me to the core. We both took some deep breaths as the car came to a stop on a gravel car park beside a lovely black and white Cheshire style building. We got out of the car and walked towards the main road.

And there he was. Jamie. The reason why we'd stopped. I looked at him with new eyes, not the shocked eyes of my younger self. He looked warn and tired, but also grubby and rough around the edges. I watched and felt the pain of the conversation. It was hellish watching – like *Big Brother* only you're the only person in it. I knew all about the attraction, the past, the history and the nostalgic ties. The horrible realisation that the family you had created and loved had been smashed to bits, brutally right in front of your eyes. My past self was not as clinical or as calm. Jamie was self assured – confident and very definitely aware of the power he could bring to bare. I moved away as the discussion turned toward the children and plans were made.

Suddenly, I had to rush to catch up as Jamie and young Helena walked towards the black and white house - the Bail Hostel. I'd forgotten this part, probably on purpose. After Jamie's arrest and the trauma of the Police search I had been asked if Jamie could return to the family home. It had been a heartbreaker of a decision, but it wouldn't have done any of us any good. It was broken, destroyed and there was no more patching up to be done. So I said no and this was the first real contact since that fateful day.

The door of the Bail Hostel swung open and the institutionalised smell and grim surroundings hit me for the second time. I watched Jamie write down a telephone number and mutter some arrangements. How had it come to this? There was the slight edge of resentment from Jamie after refusing to have him back, but it was the only way to survive. None of this was what I wanted.

The very hardest thing about watching this scene is seeing the longing still there in my young face – the inability to accept that the whole thing was a shambles and the courage to walk away for good. I knew how overpowering and devastating this meeting had been for me. Watching myself get back in the old battered Bessie – my world again on its knees.

I stopped myself from getting into the car. The journey and letdowns from Jamie that followed were old news to me and I had no desire to watch it all play out.

I especially didn't want to experience the cruel emotional blows that Jamie's behaviour would have on my two girls – once was more than enough.

That's when I decided to take a different tack. What was the worst thing that could happen? Get sent back to my pod? That would happen anyway.

So instead of following my own sorry self and sharing the pain that that Jamie would continue to cause. I decided to follow him.

Jamie stood for while as the car drove away. He sighed deeply and then lit a rather grubby, and rather dubious, roll up that he had been saving from behind his ear. He inhaled deeply and kicked at the shale beneath his feet. Then it was as if a switch had been flicked. A voice called him and another 'inmate' walked across the car park. He wasn't a first timer, I thought to myself noting the missing teeth, yellow stained fingers and the hard stubbly contours of his face. They muttered together about a forthcoming card game and Jamie began laughing as he told some jokes. Jamie had switched off his past life, just as he had always been able to do. I had never ever known Jamie have a sleepless night or worry about anything for longer than a few minutes. It suddenly dawned on me watching him laugh and joke and share weed with his dodgy mates that he had no conscience. I'd always thought it – but could now see it so clearly – there was no jiminy cricket to save Jamie. His conscience had never been activated.

'What in God's name do you think you're doing?' Flint's voice cut across the car park. 'You are meant to be in the car with Helena! Jamie is not on trial here. We are attempting to sort out the sorry state of affairs in your head.'

'Yes well. Thanks for that. I sort of know now.....'

'Time to go Helena ! This is NOT a pick and mix experience. We send you and you stay with yourself!! You leave us no choice but to monitor you. Fantastic work Helena. '

A crackle and a flash of light and into oblivion.

'*Jailhouse Rock*'
Elvis Presley

'**Y**ou really do need to stay on track Helena. Please remember that we send you to those locations for a reason.' Pink said under her breath. 'We've got rather a rush on and as *your* Plenni team are all on double sessions – well it's put rather a strain on the main frame.'

'I never asked to go twice..' I replied

'No, but you do know that it is unacceptable to just wander off!'

'Don't molly coddle her Pink! Back you go Helena and *do not* wander off or we may have to leave you there in that sad old life of yours.'

The light crackled and fizzed and back I went. My body felt pressured and my head pounded – I think it was too soon.

I blinked and shook my head as the light blurred and the sounds slurred around me. I closed my eyes and waited until the scene came back into focus. I sat on a bench back to back with my former self and my two girls. It took a moment to try and fix the time period – judging by my tear stained face and the age of the girls I figured it was just after the trial. Jamie had not received a custodial sentence, which was a miracle. There was no intent to harm - he just wanted his tools back out of a disgruntled customer's shed. Setting fire to the shed door was just plain idiocy. Jamie got off with community service and the Barrister had kept in touch with me throughout. He'd gone to stay at his sister's house and you can imagine how delighted I was to hear that he'd started to socialise and get out and about. How very nice for him to be a free man with no responsibilities. What a relief that he had started going to parties again whilst we faced repossession and debt collectors! Bitter, your damn right I was bitter and I didn't need anyone to tell me that it wasn't healthy to feel that way.

The girls and I were sat in the centre of the pedestrianised shopping centre which was clean and well looked after. The small town had a friendly feel to it and it had been ideal for young children. Even now I missed it, I knew I missed it and this scene with my children showed why – because I'd missed out on them! I was annoyed because the stress of surviving and dealing with Jamie's compulsive gambling, lying and disappearing had taken time away from my girls. I did my best of course, but I always feel that I never had the chance to enjoy them due to the sheer scale of the damage caused. Apparently most parents feel like that, maybe I just got mislead by the ideal, the image rather than the reality. They should still have had two parents that was the plan– this catastrophe was never part of the bigger picture.

The girls ate their cheese and onion pasties, their hair still wet from the morning swim. The tell tale bulge of books in the shopping bags indicated that the library had also been visited which meant of course that it was Saturday morning. Young Helena seemed even more distracted than usual. I knew that round about this time I had been to the Citizen's advice Bureau regarding the debts and I knew we'd lose the house. But the fight seemed to have left me and I looked very weary and disheartened.

I wracked my brains, but just couldn't quite remember what happened next – which probably meant that it was bad, very bad. The girls squabbled and ran around for a while and then I saw *him*. I wanted to block the view from my younger self. Dammit! I knew now how this played out! I should have realised from where we were sitting. There was nothing I could do.

The man was carefully locking the door of one of the black and white panelled buildings. His suit rather tired and creased, but suggesting a certain level of self importance. He walked steadily towards us and I winced as I saw myself recognise him and move in.

The man in question was the editor of the local newspaper who had published around 15 pieces of my work. I got free entrances into attractions and theme parks, he got a family report of the trip. There was no money involved, but it gave my girls free days out to some of the theme parks and the zoo and gave me some valuable published work for my Creative Writing course. At this time in my life, my dream was to write feature articles for a magazine. I had loved writing the articles and we had had some great times. There had been some family photographs taken to accompany the pieces so that readers would follow the family's adventures. I wrote a quite detailed description of each place, described the location, amenities, cost and entertainment value. The children also gave the attraction a star rating and loved being involved. Sometimes people recognised us as the family from the paper. But as with everything else that involved Jamie – this too had been ruined. Not for the reason that you may think –ie. that Jamie could no longer participate. No, I had accepted that a long time ago. This was worse, deeper and would change the course of my life.

Damn! I hadn't been concentrating. My younger self was up and away and approaching the editor ready for battle. I didn't want to hear the actual conversation again – I hadn't forgotten. I did however want to watch the editor, as the red mist of anger had prevented me from doing this at the time. Luckily the girls stayed put as two very different Helena's approached the hack. My younger version was shaken, but wanted answers as to why this editor had used one of the photographs used in my article to accompany a piece about Jamie going to court charged with arson. Young Helena kept asking why had he used the photograph, albeit without the three of us on it and why such a focus and wide coverage? Did he realise the effect it had on my children? Everyone knew us, knew he was the father of the family who did the adventures. We'd been pointed at at the school gates, gossiped about, humiliated. I'd been into school to see the Headmistress who understood after a fiasco she had once had with the press. This was a very local paper. He should never have used this photograph, it was taken with his family for a different purpose.

It was vicious and unkind and only had an effect on the innocent, as Jamie was no longer living in this area. My older self watched him wanting to study his reaction. He looked disinterested and slightly bored. Eventually he responded and said he used the photo because he had it and because he could. That's journalism! he added and turned and walked away.

No truer words could have been spoken. It was indeed journalism and to think that I had wanted to enter into this field of smears and character annihilation. He'd done me a favour. Not only had I found out who my true friends were, but now I knew very clearly what I didn't want to do with my life. I could never have done what he had no problem doing, and I knew it. It closed a chapter of my life. We both returned to the girls who were none the wiser. My younger self gritted her teeth, her mouth set in determination as they set on their weary way home, a home which would soon be lost. Enough, I welcome the journey back to the pod which seemed for once to come immediately.

Red light spells danger
Billy Ocean

I arrived at Plenni just after Andy.

'I'd love to know who picks these tunes.' Andy said whilst perching on the edge of the table.

'I think I can hazard a guess.' I added.

'Andy, how long do you think, well do you think... you have left?'

'Don't beat about the bush lovely, straight in there! Still, as you may well be after me, I can't blame you for asking like. It's hard to say for sure, but maybe three or four Plenni. How about you?'

'Maybe five. What theme will you have for your last Plenni?'

'Hadn't really thought of it, going to be hard to beat Barry's though. That was a ball!'

The lights flickered as Berni and Shauna arrived together, swiftly followed by Brian. We all took our places at the table and automatically took our respective goodies. Shauna hummed along to Billy Ocean.

'Someone's got a bloody good sense of humour. Who's the Commandant tonight?'

'I'm afraid it's Alan.' I said as the lights flickered in agreement. 'And he's very, very nosy .'

'I thought we might play a game tonight to relieve the tension a little.'

'I can hardly control my excitement, what's it going to be, pin the tail on the Welshy or blind man's Brian?'

There was a faint flicker of laughter.

'Come on Shauna let's give it a go, after all it's not as if we can have a heart to heart with the spies listening in.'

'I'm up for it.' stated Andy. 'Well, not for letting Shauna loose with a pin anywhere near my nethers or chasing Brian around while he's blindfolded! Who invented those games for children anyway?'

'Some sadistic bastard, the same one who wrote the terrifying nursery rhymes and those Grimm stories about wolves eating little girls in red riding outfits.'

The mood lifted. Meanwhile Berni gave out paper and pencils to all of us.

'OK we're doing the clean and simple version – you don't need to be able to draw but it helps.' Berni winked.

'Do we add a caption?' I asked. Everyone sighed as if I was a moron. There must be something more to it. Then I realised that this may be the only chance we would get to communicate, due to Flint's close monitoring of this Plenni. I nodded to show that I understood. Shauna shot me a patronising glance.

'Now without further ado. It's very simple and can be fun if everyone plays properly, no paper airplanes like the one that Andy's just made.' said Berni, as Andy then threw his plane across the table.

'The wings are very complex on that, should have been a template for a British Aerospace design.' Shauna yawned as the paper plane landed near her, it only took her a second to spot the writing under the wing.

She cleverly flipped it on its side and made the pretence of showing it to Brian.

'Have you seen this before, or is it a design that boys are taught along with writing their names in the snow with piss!'

At first Brian ignored her as usual and then realised he was missing the point. He read the message and threw it back pretending to aim at Andy but it came to me instead.

'Pathetic ! It doesn't even go in a straight line!' said Brian. I casually flipped the paper plane over and read, *All messages on back of Berni's sheet ONLY – less of a risk.* Berni was the only one who hadn't seen it dammit!

'Children children! Stop wasting time. Helena give me the plane.' She grabbed the plane and screwed it up. I had no choice I knocked the water off the table and the glass landed near her foot.

'I'm sorry Berni – let me get that.' As I had hoped we both reached down together and I had a split second to tell her, 'messages on yours only!' I whispered.

'I know.' she hissed back. Some people were just more perceptive than I am and that's all there was to it!

'Now attention class! We've had the aeroplane and the water fight now behave! It's very simple...'

Shauna began to giggle.

'There's always one! If you can't behave then you won't play and I don't think that's what you really want.'

Uncharacteristically Shauna piped down. 'Now everyone takes a sheet of paper and at the top of it draws the head either of a person, an animal or a bird. Then the sheet must be folded so the drawn head can't be seen, except a little part of the neck. Then this drawing is passed to the player next to them. Now everyone draws the body then folds the paper and again passes it to the player next to them. Then the legs then the feet. Then we unfold the picture and see what we have. It's a bit babyish but should be fun. Time is of the essence here. Off we go.'

Everyone conforms. Occasionally there is a pause, when Berni's paper marked with a cross on the bottom corner reaches them. Finally, the mission is complete and the unfolding begins. Berni states that she can chose to go last as it's her game. There are a few whoops and shouts of 'spoilty pants' just to keep the spirit of the game going. Normally this would have been great fun, but we all knew the stakes were high. There is much hilarity, but we are all desperate to know what the underlying messages say. Berni shows her contribution last as everyone votes for a winner and we all dutifully vote for her.

'I get to pass it round and get it signed as I'm the winner and there are no prizes.' brags Berni.

'How old are you?' asks Shauna. 'Jesus, James and Mary were you spoilt as a child by any bleeding chance?' Shauna does a half smile to show that she's staying in character. Everyone thanks Berni for the game and messes about, talking over one another while the paper is passed around and the message on the back is read by all. Then everyone makes a big play of shredding their efforts including Berni's. It was important to destroy it completely or everything would have been lost.

Suddenly Alan's voice cuts across like a knife.

'Early bed time for naughty children. You have two minutes to say goodbye – part of your punishment and also because I can't watch or listen to any more of this inane banter. It made my nails curl, what is the world, even this semi conscious world, coming to? At least charades would have been a shade more entertaining! I suspect it may have been too intellectually challenging for some of you! Make haste!'

'He's such a charmer.' smiled Brian. 'Shall we?'

'Not the group hug! Positively nauseating. I feel like I'm watching an Oprah Winfrey re-run!' We hugged knowingly and nods of agreement went discreetly around the group.

'Until next time.' said Berni.

'I'm going to swap my shift with Keith Chegwin – watching his group of losers can't be any worse than this!'

Paper Moon
Nat King Cole

I woke up, aware that I needed to keep my head clear. Mercifully I wasn't being monitored or told about my next visit – for now at least. Dare I think about it now? Should I wait until I went back – something was niggling at me.

'Good morning Helena. You should be pleased to know the next one isn't too bad. Well, for one of your visits it's not too bad. Flint told me it was like kindergarten last night at Plenni – he's even put in a request to avoid the next few. Wonderful! Well I've had a lovely days break and I'm happy to give you a little time to compose yourself as a little treat. Flint is torturing some other victim so go ahead and enjoy a quiet 5 minutes.'

I hesitated and then began humming tunelessly as I quickly worked through the messages in my head. I visualised the piece of paper and hurried scribbles in order to remember and to keep the memory.

1. **Shauna** – *Big repair on our block - Mel let it slip -not sure when*
2. **Brian** – *Brad said he was taking leave in few weeks buildings need maintenance*

3. **Andy** – *We can do lights but can we undo magnetic lock on inner door and we don't know what's outside*
4. **Me** – *Time limited - guides need pressuring for info. Feel need to work on external connection between us and our location.*
5. **Berni** – *need time to push guides and instinct tells me there is a greater plan which we will have to work out. Normal Plenni needed.*

That was a lot to work on and I knew Pink would be back any minute. I shut the file in my head and mentally locked it away. Just in time.

'It's time Helena. This one should be easier.' announced Pink just as the lights began to flicker. My heart wasn't in it, but there was no choice. My eyes opened and adjusted slowly to the yellow fluorescence of the strip lights. I could sense the tension in the room. Everyone was sat around an oval oak table and it was then I remembered where I was. Court. County Court, to be precise, at my divorce hearing. Jamie had not showed up, even though a private detective had located him and he had been served. No surprise there. He never fought for any of us – coward. I looked at my younger self, pale, thin but determined. My solicitor was reading through a long list of events where Jamie had let me down or the girls or got himself into trouble with the authorities. It went on and on and I realised for the first time, in a long time, that I didn't want to hear it any more. I'd lived it, felt the pain of it and no longer wanted to think about it! This was an amazing breakthrough! Months of gruelling counselling and 'empowering' discussions had not lead me to this place. Jamie had taken enough from me, no more. Even my former self looked a tad disillusioned – probably sick of hearing what a shit he was. There was one very important part of this meeting though and one which I remembered, but not unfondly. And if my memory served me right it was about to happen.

The judge, wearing just a normal suit, but clearly a man not to be trifled with, began to look increasingly uncomfortable. My solicitor, Miss Davidson, a confident and candid professional was outlining the details of Jamie's desertion. She explained how he'd gone out to get a pint of milk and never came back. That was about 18 months ago. How the court had appointed a private investigator to find him as I was unable to sell the house as it was in joint names. It was a case of selling the wonderful 4 bedroom home, which we all loved, before it was repossessed. The mortgage company were unable to let me sell without a court order, even though the house was in negative equity. The solicitor reeled off more evidence regarding Jamie's behaviour and his unreliable word and pointed out his absence in court again. I could feel the anger rising as I remembered the unfairness of being left with the gambling debts, now losing our home and having no money and of course having 2 girls to raise. I glanced across to see how I was doing – no sign of anger just a thin, worn face and tired resignation. I was about to lose the only security we had left and the burden was a heavy one. What a complete and utter shit. I remember that I used to pray to win the lottery or get an offer on a book deal which would save us, but it never came. The social security benefit didn't cover the mortgage as we had remortgaged to pay off Jamie's debts at least twice. He'd lost his job many times, 8 times in 5 years. Good jobs, well paid jobs with company cars and high salaries, but was unable or unwilling to conform to the requirements of the job. The mortgage company had been fair giving me time to sell, but even when a buyer had been secured, which let me tell you was absolutely heart breaking, we couldn't sell as I didn't know where Jamie was and of course he hadn't been in contact or sent any money.

The judge seemed to shrink down in his seat and his lips pursed angrily as Miss Davidson related incidents regarding the girls and Jamie's neglect.

'Enough! I have heard enough. Sign it off Miss Davidson. The divorce will go through –list desertion and mental cruelty as the grounds. I believe that the plaintiff has agreed to divorce.' Miss Davidson nodded.

'Regarding the property, it shall be sold and the mortgage company are permitted to accept a sole signature should Mr Collins disappear again. This family must be allowed to move forward and the financial burden of the negative equity will fall to Mr Collins - which it didn't by the way. This should suffice, counsel will keep me informed.' With that the judge rose as did everyone else as he left the room. Miss Davison patted my hand. 'That's the end of it, we got what we need.' It's funny I never remembered thanking her, it must have been the shock. But now I watched my young self thank her and get a lift home with her, which I had totally forgotten.

It was dreadful, the whole thing – but somehow I had managed not to become totally immersed in the emotional showdown. This was unbelievable progress as though I had been able to watch and listen as it was all in the past now. This chapter in my life could now be closed as I watched myself leave.

God knows how or why, but my survival mode had suddenly, finally kicked in and my underlying concern now was not for the past, but for the future. The escape of not only me, but my friends in Plenni. The powerful pull of wanting to find a way out and understand not only where we were, but what our futures would hold was overwhelming. My past was awful and the scars would always be there, but not at the expense of my future and the future of my family. Jamie's emotional and psychological hold over me had started to falter and the bigger picture had suddenly come into focus. The pieces had always been there, I had always loved my children and my family, but the horror of his actions had knocked me off the pathway and I had been unable to see the destination. Now it became clear and I was going to need to pull on that inner strength and gritty determination to work with the Plenni team if we were ever going to get out – that is if there is any way of getting out and anywhere to go to. But surely they wouldn't be doing this if we were just going to die? Unless it turns out to be one of those sick game shows which is just in a studio..... Oh my God! Where did that thought come from!! I had to get it out of my head!! Quick... Think brick wall...

'It's time to return Cinderella - the pumpkin awaits. No glass slipper I'm afraid. I would really appreciate some time off away these tedious domestic battles.'

'You must never think of taking up a career in counselling Flint!'

'No fear my dear Helena. No fear at all. The pod awaits you.. Sweet dreams.'

Good Morning Judge
10cc

I was really hoping that Flint had kept his promise and taken some time off, but judging by the choice of song it could only have been him.

'You're right of course, well in one way.' Pink butted into my head, something she hadn't done for a while.

'Pink do you mind? I have asked you not to just jump straight into my head, I do need a place to retreat to!'

'Of course, my mistake, it's just so easy to comment directly. My sincerest apologies. I thought you'd be pleased to know that Flint has taken two days R and R. So I will be monitoring you, lightly of course, as your guide that is.' Pink faltered.

'Well, as you've brought such good news, I'll let you off.'

'Thank you. You seem quite unaffected by yesterday's court scene – Oh and you were quite right Flint organised your wake up song before he took his leave.'

'I knew it! Thanks Pink. And no I'm not strung out over the court room drama, I think I'm getting a bit tired of going over old ground and dwelling on the past. I know that my girls have moved forward and my family most definitely have. I don't want to be the one left dwelling over the shadows of old memories, unable to let go. '

'I'll just say this Helena, think of your theme, sometimes it's important to think about things from a different perspective.' and with that she clicked off.

My theme was 'Leaving'. I'd never given it much thought, confident that it referred to me being left – at different stages of my life. But maybe I could change things, maybe I could focus on me leaving my past!! Me moving forward and moving away from the pain instead of me looking back at being left!

I felt slightly dizzy – I checked that the oxygen pipe had not come lose, the light headedness quickly passed. Oh my God – maybe everyone should think about their themes!! And also about what had happened to each of us before we came here.

I took a deep breath which coincided with my entrance to Plenni. The journey was becoming quicker and less unsettling. For some reason I was the last to arrive.

'About bloody' time!' muttered Andy. Everyone was seated around the table and demolishing the goodies. I took my place and asked what I'd missed.

'We were just thinking about Andy's party and writing a list of ideas.'

'God that's a bit premature I mean… youch!' Shauna trod down on my little toe.

'Jese Louise – get a bloody grip Helena!'

'So moving on.' interrupted Brian. 'Berni is taking the notes and we all add to it as we go on.'

'Now about Point 2 off last week's agenda regardin' the rooming.' I chewed on my vitamin lozenge, anxious to keep quiet and get up to speed.

'As far as I know we can use the Collective's computer via our guides in order to set the scene.' Brian paused and then under his breath said 'Two weeks max until the builders are in.'

'Funny that two weeks max and I'll have the painters in!' joked Shauna. We both began laughing, Berni frowned and Brian went a little pale.

'Lovely. Thank you for your contribution regarding your menstrual cycle Shauna.'

'Seriously though I concur.'

'Oh you concur, well how dashingly lovely!' mocked Shauna.

'Anyhow, this room will look great! And ... I know my theme!'

'Yay!.' Shauna yelled and everyone applauded.' Let's guess! Shaun the sheep!'

'Are you going to star as Tom Jones! Can I be Shirley Bassey.'

'Will there be a Welsh male voice choir singing in the background?' asked Brian.

'Poor Andy, such small minded views.' Berni said quietly.

Andy pretended to look cross and then smiled.

'They mean it kindly Berni, no worries. Anyhow Tommo is very popular with the women folk so I'll take that as a compliment!'

'Come on then tell us!!! For God's sake.'

'Well I think some of you will be a little surprised by my choice, but if I've gotta go, then so be it. I want my leaving party to be in the style of ... *The Rocky Horror Show*.' Shauna was the first to laugh and I hid my smile quite well, I thought. Berni tutted at Shauna.

'Well I'm not sure what it is but even if I do have to take part in a Canadian slasher theme –if it's what Andy wants I'm up for it.'

Shauna lost control and I took Berni to one side and explained the basic storyline and the musical content.

Brian wriggled uncomfortably on his seat and looked forlorn.

'Andy mate – it's your show an' all but I just can't, well, I just can't wear suspenders.'

'That's OK Bri, I'll take care of that role. I will be Dr. Frank-N-Furter.'

'There's only one role for me and that's Magenta Right Andy?'

'Yes yes of course – I already had you in mind for that Shauna. Helena would you be Janet Weiss? Brian you can be Brad – in normal blokes clothing of course and Berni could you be Columbia or as she's known little Nell?'

'You do know Berni that Columbia is a groupie!' laughed Shauna

'Well if that's what Andy wants for his leaving do – I can oblige.' Berni smiled and we all laughed.

'Come on guys it'll be a great laugh and the music is brilliant!'

We all followed Andy's lead and put our hands on top of each others in a clumsy pile and let out an almighty roar.

'Thanks so much – it gives me something, well something to look forward to.' He dropped his voice. 'Can we try and move the bolt a little way – now our hands are together?'

'Let's do the one potato, two potato game.' I said and we started messing about piling our hands on top of each other and singing.

'One potato, two potato, three potato four....

'On the next count of four.' Berni said quietly. Berni kept singing, we all closed our eyes and there was the sound of a metallic squeak. 'We moved it just a little.' Berni said under her breath.

'High fives all round for Andy's theme!' announced Brian.

'Yeah themes are such fun.' I paused, here was my chance. Under my breath I murmured, 'I think there's something in the themes, maybe a connection or double meaning. Also, I think that there must be a way of blowing the electrics to make sure everything is shut down and not electronically locked. Bri that's your department.' There was a nod and a wink, a knowing look which showed I had been understood. Just in time as the lights flickered and back we went.

Time warp
The Rocky Horror Picture Show.

'And before you ask Helena, no Flint is not back and yes I did choose this song - admittedly I had to ask Richard Branson for a little help, but I'm quite proud of myself.'

'Great Pink.' I yawned. 'I know you're excited at selecting a 'modern song'. Thanks. But I've asked you before to stop jumping straight into my head, it's just downright rude.'

'Yes, you're quite right of course. I got a little carried away with myself. I'm sorry Helena.'

'That's OK and by the way the *Rocky Horror film* was made in 1975 so it's not actually that modern. But, Flint would have been proud of your effort. Even though it means that Plenni is still being spied on and we have no privacy. Well done.'

'Aah, Yes, well I never really thought about it from that perspective.'

'Pink, could I ask you something while the storm trooper is away?'

'You may ask Helena, but I may not answer.'

'I was just wondering whether anyone had ever escaped, in the time you've been here, I mean.'

'Time is ticking on. Even if I knew, I couldn't possibly tell you. Now we mustn't get behind or you'll be late for Plenni.'

Pink clicked off. Ah well it was worth a try. I was getting tired of being thrust back into the past, as I had started to focus on the future. I felt my heart sink as I opened my eyes onto yet another episode of my life. But somehow it was less intense now and I felt more detached from it at long last! Counselling had not achieved this distance and dumbing down of the connection to my memories and past life.

I wearily opened my eyes struggling to muster some interest or enthusiasm, until that is I caught site of my broken self.

'I'll watch this – then I want to move forward!' I spoke forcefully out loud, watching my past self as slowly I dialled the solicitors number on the telephone.

'Yes I know that the private investigator has found him! Look, I just want to know where he is! You told me to have the weekend as a cooling off period. I've done that even though it's been tough. So please, after months and months of not knowing I really think I have the right to know!'

I couldn't hear what the solicitor said, but I knew she was trying to calm me down, afraid I may react or retaliate in some way.

'Yes I am calm. For almost 2 years I thought he was dead or in Australia or prison – now what could possibly be worse? Gina, for God's sake just tell me!'

I know exactly what she said, Jamie was living 10 miles from where we lived. But that was only the first shock. I remember the hesitancy in the solicitor's voice as she stalled before telling me the rest of it. He wasn't living there alone, he was living with a woman who worked in the estate agents, where he had gone to find somewhere to live. I watched my reaction. It was weird to see it, as all I could remember was feeling it. Shock ran through me as my young face blanched and I sat down abruptly on a dining chair. There was relief he was alive, edged with the horror of knowing that he could have seen the girls, but worse than that he was living with another woman. I followed myself into the kitchen where I knew I would light a cigarette before phoning my parents and Jamie's sisters. The shaking hand and ravaged face said it all. I had seen enough, after all I'd lived it once before.

The screen crackled as I move to the next location. I was sat in the back of my own car- my good friend driving as we set off to find Jamie's house. My friend, Lucy, had agreed she would go to the door and speak with Jamie and ask him to contact me. By the look of the countryside I knew we were almost there and again I knew what was coming. I felt immediate pain as I looked at my drawn, tired face which had been carefully made up to mask the fear. My friend parked up back of a row of cottages. In the garden of the middle house, hung a line of washing and some children's clothes. My friend pre-empted me.

'We don't know it's that house. He's hardly likely to take on a load of kids when he couldn't cope with his own.' Lucy reassured me.

'I'm going now.' She squeezed my hand and set off to the house. Inevitably, I lit a cigarette. I wished I had one right now, I thought to myself. Lucy returned within minutes but it felt like hours.

'A woman answered the door – she was wrapped in a sheet. I don't know if Jamie was there, but she said she would get him to call you.'

I could hear her describing the woman and the house – but there was only one thing I wanted to know and she knew it. My past self turned and looked her straight in the eye and without saying a word, Lucy answered the silent question.

'I saw pink t shirts on the radiator and children's jackets hung on the banister – probably about 7 or 8 years old.' Lucy looked away.

This had been my worst nightmare – all along I had believed that whatever had happened Jamie would never have lived with someone else's children whilst neglecting his own in such a brutal way. All the questions I could never answer, all the presents they'd never had, the hugs they'd longed for and the hours waiting by the window. What a complete and utter shit!!!

In the years that had past, along with my own personal rejection of course, this was one of the hardest things I'd had to bear. My own shattered heart was one thing to cope with, but the pain of my children was beyond agony. Shock managed to numb the young Helena. The familiar wave of sickness and disgust went through me, as I saw a sadness and flicker of defeat cross my face and linger in the eyes. Then it was gone and with the help of dear Lucy we pushed on home. I knew then, that once I had approached Jamie, he would contact me and the girls. He had no damn right of course! But it wasn't my decision to make. Other people went through this and worse – I knew that, but I just couldn't believe Jamie would live with and support someone else's children, whilst willfully neglecting his own for such a long time. I've always believed that not knowing is worse than knowing and not knowing if someone is alive or dead is beyond cruel not only to me, but to any child. God may forgive him, but I'm not sure I ever will. There are programmes on TV about men or women who go out to the local shop and never come back. Both then and now I still cannot believe that it had had happened to me! Maybe these things are always unreal to the people they happen to. One thing for sure - I didn't want to spend a minute longer thinking about it and I wasn't prepared to. I could feel myself detaching from the past and there was the stirring of a fire in my belly to push on with the future. It was time for me to leave, at long last a time to move on.

'Pink! I want to go now! I've seen enough...'

Nothing happened.

'Pink! Please can I go back now!'

As I shouted once again I saw a slight reaction from young Helena, she seemed to almost flinch. As I filled my lungs to shout again, the familiar crackling began and I as transferred back to the pod – fully conscious for once and ready to move on. My decision at last!! And boy does it feel good!!!

Move on up
M people

'Still spying on people then? Not got enough entertainment in your own sad little lives that you have to listen into ours? I'm surprised at you though Pink. I thought that Flint was the chief persecutor in the camp!'

'How little she knows' snarled Flint.

'I should've known you were back. It's not Pink's style.'

'For someone who normally returns from each episode in an unconscious state, I find your cynicism somewhat irksome.'

'I really hope that I can be present when they unpick your life and play it back to you! Maybe I can a produce a DVD which reflects **your** darkest hours! What fun!!'

'Someone got up on the wrong side of their pod this morning...'

'Honestly you two, it's just like kindergarten.' interrupted Pink.

'I think I'm justified – I really do. When am I getting out of here Pink? That is if anyone ever does get out of here. For God's sake !! Haven't I done enough? Seen enough! Been through enough!!'

'It's time for Plenni Helena.' Pink said coolly. 'There are things happening here that you just don't understand, well, can't understand– it would be better if you just complete the series of episodes and concentrate on addressing your theme. There is nothing more I'm prepared to say, now for the moment you must go to Plenni and as you managed to return to us with your mind intact – I think we can assume that progress has been and is being made.'

'Slowly, slowly catchee monkey, that's always your way Pink. Run along now dear sweet Helena and play with your friends.'

'You're quite insane Flint ! Hans Gruber lives on. And may I point out that we can't actually leave, Flint, so I will run along and meeting my friends in Plenni!'

'Little Miss Dramatic aren't we? One look at your Plenni comrades confirms the unsuitability and unlikelihood of your group ever being acknowledged or accepted together in the real world.'

'So there is a world outside this bizarre existence? Don't you think it's time that you told me, even just a snippet, after all I must be coming to the end now. I don't need to go back any more ! I get it, I understand - let the past go, move forward and grab life by the balls! Lesson learnt'

'How charming. But as delightful as this conversation has been I simply must dash and share in some other poor deluded cell mates' 'journey'.' Flint clicked off. I knew that this was my only chance with Pink.

'Please Pink, give me something, anything that can give us hope.'

'You'll see soon enough Helena. My hands are tied as you well know. All I can say is that your journey is almost complete. There's no need to fear, you will see and very soon.' And with that there was the familiar snap, crackle and pop as I was launched into Plenni.

I was first to arrive and carefully began to examine my surroundings with a very different agenda on my mind. The bland, whitewashed walls with the dim down lighters had nothing to offer, as far as electrics went. But I could hear the familiar throb of the lift type Musak and knew it had to have an outlet somewhere in the room, even if it was only in the form of speakers. There was also the massive screen which was the portal between all the various pods, but that would take some technical expertise which I didn't have and if anything went wrong, could jeopardise our very survival – if indeed we were actually alive. I looked across the table as the familiar sounds of my group's arrival distracted me. I had never been in a fit state, or had the opportunity, to watch everyone arrive before. The shimmering whirlpools of light came almost simultaneously. The silver sparkles turned to colour and then the form of the person came into view. It was so close to a Star Trek moment, when Spok says energize and Jim returns from some god forsaken planet.

'Good Lord, you're barking mad girl and they say TV doesn't damage the mind!' Flint bounced his comment into my head, reminding me that we were going to have to be extremely careful. Pink was no soft touch, but she didn't interfere anywhere near as much.

'That's because you're both women, 'drawn' together by the weird sisterhood, delivering each other's babies and gathering herbs from under the oak tree to turn toads into princes. Balderdash!' and with that Flint clicked off. To be honest I was becoming less able to detect his presence or hear any of the sounds which used to alert me to his presence – we were going to have to be vigilant and who knew whether or not the other guides would decide to listen in to entertain themselves. The familiar stir of anxiety coupled with a sense of urgency hit the pit of my stomach.

We quickly went through the usual pleasantries. I noticed that everyone was much quieter than usual.

'Andy, how many sessions you got left?' Shauna whispered .

Andy looked down and I knew we had to get moving on our plan.

'Two maybe three, they don't tell you...'

'I feel it could be three, but it depends on how you're doing with your sessions Andy.' Berni said quietly.

'I've been thinking about our costumes, it's only an idea. Most of the women and Frank N Furter wear stilettos and there's a lot of sequins and buttons and elastic – could we use them somehow to fuse the electrics? We'd have to use our collective power to slide the bolt on the door first of course.'

'Fuckin' mint idea – I'm clueless with electrics - Brian and Andy could have that as their project.'

I sensed a presence and knew that Flint was near, as he always seemed to be when I spoke out. I winked at Berni who immediately got my drift.

'Well as I have no idea what this *horror Rococo* is about, maybe Shauna and Helena could enlighten me whilst Andy and Brian draw up the materials er.. costume lists.'

'I'm no expert on the electrics, but I did go to a spate of Rocky Horror theme parties when I was a student, so I know the costumes.'

'I've got a very basic grasp of circuitry.' Brian said under his breath.

'Let's get goin' then before the bastards blast us back to the pods!' Shauna said excitedly.

We split quickly into 2 groups, which I was relieved about as it would be less easy to monitor our every word. Shauna and I outlined the plot of 'Rocky Horror' for Berni who looked on incredulously.

'Good grief, who thought up this weird and sexually depraved musical? I don't really think it qualifies as a musical unless they have special section for murderous musicals!'

'It was written by the bloke off *The Crystal Maze,* can't think of his bleedin' name.'

'Richard O'Brien.' I responded.

Berni looked a little stunned.

'It's OK, it's just dressing up and bit of dancing.' She smiled weakly.

'Look Berni I don't think we've got long. Flint said something strange, not unusual I know – but he was having a go at the sisterhood and got quite animated about me and Pink having some women's bonding thing going. It isn't the case, although she is a little more sympathetic. But anyway while the boys are busy designing, could we have a go at trying out our collective female power. Just in case it makes a difference?'

'It gets weirder in here by the fuckin' minute.' stated Shauna.

'We must do it now, time is running out. Hands under the table quickly!'

'Jesus this looks dodgy, I'm feeling positively fuckin' weirded out.'

'Shauna be quiet – concentrate on moving the spare chair it's got a metal frame – we can't risk the bolt or the screen.'

I looked over at Andy before closing my eyes – he raised the pitch of his voice talking loudly about Frank N Furter's suspenders.

There was a strange prickling in my hands and I knew the power was coming from Berni. I didn't want Shauna to block the connection so I elbowed her lightly and she steeled herself in concentration.

We all jumped when the chair fell over!

'Christ alive!' shouted Shauna.

Brian was closest to the chair and jumped up.

'Sorry to make you jump Shauna I just caught it with my foot when we were stepping out the *Time Warp* dance.'

'Well take a step to the right and then a jump to the left!'

Come on everybody –up you bloody get – it's rehearsal time. Everyone got up, glad of the rest bite, even Berni.

'Here we go...' Everyone was up and doing their best to join in.

It's just a jump to the left And then a step to the right With your hands on your hips You bring your knees in tight'

The air crackled and the bright light filled the room, as back we went.

Touch-a, Touch-a, Touch-a, Touch me
Janet Weiss

It was great to arrive back to the pod alert and awake, I must be getting stronger. I began humming along to the music trying to keep my mind free of any subversive thoughts.

'Nicely done Helena, progress is definitely being made.'

'How lovely, another bonding session for the female duo. And as far as 'The Rocky Horror Show' goes I think it's a superb metaphor for most of your lives.'

'That's a tad bitchy Flint and they say women can be cruel! I have a question for you Flint, I'm not expecting an answer, but as I have nothing to lose.'

'Yes, what would you like to know apart from how to get your sorry little self out of here.' he said.

'When you were in 'Truly Madly Deeply' and you were a ghost, I know you were only acting, but it was quite an emotional role for you...'

'Why can't women just ask a question? What is it you would like to know?'

'You played it with such feeling and in the end you left your girlfriend, so that she could move on with her life.'

'I do know the film Helena.'

'Well all I was going to ask is if you can you see a connection with this situation, do you have any empathy for any of us.'

'Ah, (pause) No. That was a film for chrissakes! I don't live in the forest just because I had a part in Robin Hood, I don't live in a castle and behave like Severus Snape – I'm not the cheating husband out of *Love Actually* – Helena I am an actor!! I have been chosen by you as a guide, God alone knows why! Pink deal with this rambling girl I have far bigger fish to fry.'

'I'm unclear as to what you hope to achieve Helena, but you have successfully raised his dander.'

'Good, then he knows how it feels, although I'm not sure we have a dander we can raise!'

I could hear Dame Judi's wicked giggle and smiled to myself, things were changing I could feel it.

'If we could just leave danders to one side ladies and address ourselves to the job in hand.'

It was my turn to giggle and Pink clicked herself off for a moment.

'Right, enough! I'm just sending her Pink, enough of the giggly girlie approach!'

And with that I was transported back into my tawdry past, but something had shifted and I was ready for whatever I had to watch.

I opened my eyes and we were all in the park. Of course it would have to be 'the meeting.' Ugh, I inwardly sighed, once was enough. For the very first time I wondered if I could just go back to my pod. Just this once, after all I had been back many times. I closed my eyes and tried to will myself back. Nothing happened. I watched my weary, worn, past self reassure my two girls as we made our way into the forest. Sammy made me smile as she ran around enthusiastically, always a nature lover and an outdoor girl. Ellen was more for friends and games and also more upset by change. This meeting had been set up after I had discovered where Jamie was and he had actually phoned the house and spoken. For months he had been putting the phone down on us – I know this because I asked him if it was him that kept ringing. He wanted to see the girls and I asked them if they wanted to see him. It was and always has been their choice – he's not my father. We'd agreed to me at a nearby park and I'd asked him to come alone. After a short wait, he was there leaning against a tree as if nothing had happened. He looked older, scruffier, but appeared confident and smiled at his children. Sammy went straight to him and Ellen just stayed close to me, uncertain and clearly nervous. I took a moment to look at my old self, run ragged, distressed and emotionally worn down. Jamie made his usual effort to run around and get the girls engaged – he was very good at this for short periods if the girls were right in front of his face. So convincing and engaging, but no staying power and definitely no regret or emotional conscience. Ellen looked uncomfortable and uncertain, the meeting unsettled her. Sammy continued to run and hide and play.

I felt a tiredness wash over me. We'd all moved on from this place, from this sadness, these heart wrenching memories needed putting firmly in their place. We were damaged and for a long time, but we have moved on, we are moving on. Maybe I'm the last to leave it behind me. The breaking of the vows, the bond, the love, the tie

I always believed was sacred between two parents and their children. It was time to let him go.

I felt rather faint as if something had been removed from me, like giving birth when the baby is expelled from you and you feel empty and start shaking. I was so sure that we would be together forever and our children would be loved and nurtured by us both. The dream shattered in front of my very eyes. Single parenthood was waiting and divorce was on its tail. Time to grow up as my children had had to.

I watched as my old self gave Ellen a piggy back, each pale face reflecting different levels of pain. I remembered the words that I had read recently in a book a friend had lent to me by Robin Sharma.

'You will stop being a prisoner of your past. Instead you will become the architect of your future.' (*The monk who sold his Ferrari*)

I could see now in this moment that I had a choice, it was a new feeling which could release me from being trapped by memories in a disturbing chain of events. Jamie was no longer the man I'd known and loved. That Jamie would never have done these things. Compulsive addiction, lack of attachment, memory disorder, parental death – any of these or all of these had affected Jamie and his ability to forge and maintain relationships and I suddenly realised that none of these were my fault. I was 15 years old when I met him, engaged at 17 and married at 19. The dream had been mine, but this was the reality. I looked fondly at my two brave little girls who I knew would go on to do great things, despite him not because of him. He was the loser in this situation not me – it was time to turn the corner on the grief, as my children had a long time ago.

I looked across at my old self myself, feeling such empathy for the pain which would follow and the poverty and hard times. I looked into the focused angry eyes of Young Helena and tried to transmit hope and courage. For just a second, a brief whisper of a smile crossed young Helena's mouth and the hint of recognition flickered in her eyes. She hitched Ellen up tightly on her back, pursed her lips and began to run at a gallop into the trees to catch up with Sammy and Jamie. I turned around. It was their life now and my future life and grown up girls were waiting somewhere for me. This episode could re run forever, but I had seen it in it's true light and now for the very first time I wanted to leave it behind me! It was my Leaving!!!

The sun seemed to flicker and the light fade a little. A warm breeze blew across my face and a warm glow of hope seemed to spread through me, as I was very gently almost lifted back to my pod in the blink of an eye.

Looks like we made it
Barry Manilow

'How thoughtful Pink, are you a closet fan?'
'Pink! Where is the woman when you need her? You preset this mindless drivel? For the love of Satan get it off!'

I sighed as the music faded gently into the distance.

'Unlike you Flint, I still have the grace to acknowledge a breakthrough when I see it.'

'Yippe yay ay! Hardly a breakthrough in neuro science, unless little Miss Helena has split the atom or developed a cure for the common cold. So she's turned the corner, well done.'

'Does this mean I can go now? Have I completed the course? Will I graduate before Andy?'

'You're not a student Helena. And there are still a few loose ends to tie up. Andy - Frank-N -Furter will be the first to depart to pastures new.'

'Enough said on the subject Flint. Helena, that was a great session and significant progress has been made.'

'Girly bonding how simply lovely.' mocked Flint. 'It's not over until it's over.'

'Do you have children Flint?'

'That is quite clearly none of your business. We are here to sort out your muddled mess of a life not mine and you seem to forget that **you** picked me.'

'So you do have kids, more of a stick than a carrot type of father then?'

'I fear that psycho analysis is not your strength and will thank you to keep your intuitive babble to yourself. Is Plenni prepared Pink or have you been embroidering a shawl or preparing a herb poultice in my absence?'

'What a charmer, hold fast dear Pink you could easily take him.'

'This is of course very true, but time marches on.'

'Just zap her in there and stop pussy footing around.' Flint clicks off.

Pink lowers her voice, 'Helena,' she almost whispers, 'be very very careful in Plenni, you have a lot to lose. It's time to think of yourself a little. Think about what you've learnt from looking back over your own past. You're playing a dangerous game when you don't understand the risks. This Plenni will be monitored. I would seriously ask that you heed my warning.'

'Chinese whispers is for scout camp!' interrupted Flint. Helena is not the only one who should be careful!'

The lights flickered and I was jolted unceremoniously into Plenni.

'Where the fuck 'ave you bin?' Shauna yelled, clearly upset. 'Thought you'd found the tunnel and left us high and dry!'

'Don't be daft. Listen we have got to be ultra careful today. I've had a warning from both of my guides and that's never happened before. How are we going to organise this session so we can get er... complete our planning for the show?' After a slight pause Berni jumped up suddenly and gave out paper and pens.

'Everyone write down where they're up to, any new ideas for the er.... costumes and the script, dances and the like. A ten minute brain storming session and then we come back together and share the results. The first points should be targeting the performance and then, well some more technical ideas – if you see what I mean.'

'Yes.' said Brian somewhat stiltedly – 'We follow your drift.'

An eerie silence washed over Plenni as everyone jotted down their ideas as quickly as they could.

'Time's up! Pass them to me. OK thanks. No time to waste. Let's begin with Shauna first – some rather good sketches, a list of songs and a few questions. I'll just quickly pass this around so that everyone can appreciate the designs.'

She nodded and quickly put an asterisk next to the question – '*What the fuck do we do once we open the door in the pitch black and why are we going to knock the power off?*'

'Just add any alterations as we go round the circle and I'll feedback the results.'

Everyone understood what they had to do. Andy even drew a few sketches alongside Shauna's. Berni quickly got Shauna's paper back,

'Lovely, yes the design is coming along nicely. Perhaps Brian could just go over his response to the ...erm query?'

'I feel that we need to have control of the lighting, in the performance, for extra effect and impact..' then under his breath 'and to give us a bloody chance – we don't know what we're walking into.'

'Yes, good answer Brian.'

'We don't have many variables we can control, for the songs I mean, so the few original things we can alter the better.' stuttered Andy.

'Nicely put, does everyone follow? Great. Moving on. Ah I see that Brian and Andy have collaborated. More set designs which I'll pass around and one request which everyone can read for themselves.'

'*Whenever the show is, everyone must keep the silver paper that the goodies are wrapped in and get them to me, I'll need every scrap.*'

'Well that's fairly straight forward and the correct materials will be made available to you on the day Brian.'

Everyone nodded.

'Lovely. Ah mine next. You can see that I haven't done any sketches for the *Rudey Horror* costumes …'

'*Rocky Horror!* Berni, where have you been for the last twenty years?' Shauna laughed to herself and everyone smiled.

'Thank you Shauna, very helpful. I have jotted down a few queries regarding the staging.' she passed her sheet around.

Andy spoke hurriedly, 'I can see that the three women need to be in close proximity – to follow the er dance moves and that can be arranged.'

'I think the next Plenni we'll need to draw up a programme so that we can get all the timings sorted, make sure we don't miss anything out.'

'Yes that sounds perfect and after all it's just a bit of fun to celebrate Andy's sad departure, so we'll make it as good as we can.'

Everyone nodded trying to take in the hidden messages at the same time as following the main theme. 'And finally Helena.' Berni glanced over my paper and then passed it on. 'Some nice costume ideas and a few notes which everyone can read themselves.'

'I am close to end of my time here, once you get the point they're making they seem to feel you have completed God knows what. I think we should make next week the rehearsal and then go for it. Andy – does that fit with you?'

'Some lovely ideas there Helena.' said Andy, 'and yes I think all the timings should fit, Anneka hinted at my last formal session being next – then some sort of round up. Anyhow, quick rehearsal and timing check next session.'

'Lovely. Now if I could gather all the papers together – do we have a bin?' Berni was obviously concerned about getting rid of our plans.

'I've got a better idea, just a bit of fun. Copy me.'

Shauna made sure everyone had some paper in front of them and then ripped it into very small pieces. Everyone copied, knowing it was easier to follow than to question. She pushed her pile into the middle of the table and we all did the same.

'Lights dip and change to blue!' she shouted and weirdly the lights dipped and changed colour. 'Ready! Here we go.' She climbed onto the table and dragged us all up and then grabbed a handful of the shredded paper. By this time Andy and Brian were eyeing each other quizzically. 'And throw.' She launched the shredded paper in front of the now blue spot lamps and we all followed. Then Shauna did something that none of us were expecting, she began to sing with a beautiful clear voice.

'Raindrops keep falling on my head!'

After only a slight hesitation, we all joined in glad of the relief from the seriousness. Even Berni rose to the occasion and danced around humming to herself on the table top.

And just like the guy whose feet are too big for his bed
Nothin' seems to fit
Those raindrops are falling on my head, they keep falling

There's something about standing on a table and throwing paper around that still reminds me of being naughty at school.

Everyone was joining in and jumping and throwing paper and being stupid. Amazingly Shauna knew the second verse

So I just did me some talkin' to the sun
And I said I didn't like the way he' got things done
Sleepin' on the job
Those raindrops are falling on my, head they keep falling

No-one cared if we knew the words or not, the blue light caught the paper and fluttered around us as we jumped around. We came into a circle for the chorus.

Raindrops keep falling on my head
But that doesn't mean my eyes will soon be turnin' red

Crying's not for me
Cause I'm never gonna stop the rain by complainin'
Because I'm free
Nothing's worrying me.

Our arms around each other's shoulders and as we embraced for a group hug we were transported back to our pods.

Raining in my heart
Buddy Holly

It feels good to return to the pod fully conscious and smiling. It could only be Flint who would put on this tune I thought to myself.

'Your perception is simply astounding.' chipped in Flint. 'We'll see if you're as perky after your next session.'

'Nice to know that you still monitor Plenni Flint, home life a little dull is it?'

'Whenever I visit your group at Plenni, I say a small prayer of thanks that I wasn't requested by any of them, especially by Shauna, even her name makes no sense!'

'It's just as well that you weren't a popular choice then. Not to everyone's taste are we Flint?'

'Well Helena, I'm glad you seem to be on top form. Rather a delicate session for you next. I can see Flint's musical sensitivity is still intact.'

'Hi Pink. Plenni was fun. I was rather hoping I might have a little siesta after all the excitement.'

'You're on the Costa del Sombre now Helena. There's work to be done after the Plenni shenanigans. I was never convinced of the value of Plenni, at its' inception I stated my doubts...'

'Always the ray of sunshine Flint, that happy go lightly nature must have given you hours of pleasure.' I interrupted.

'We simply must move on, delightful though it is to listen to such entertaining dialogue.' stated Pink. 'This next session will be tough, just remember that you're close to the end. Are you ready Helena?'

I'd never been asked before and found it quite disconcerting.

'OK, let's do it, it can't be any worse than some of the earlier sessions.' and with that I was once again returned to my past life.

Ah yes, this was a particularly unpleasant experience and one I would rather not live through again. I eyed the oak panelled door and wondered if I could make a run for it. But then again I could get sent back here, if I don't get from this session whatever it is I'm meant to. My stomach tied in knots, I close my eyes and take a deep breath. I look around the room, at Jamie and his 'girlfriend' and the 3 dogs which run around crazily and at my two daughters one nervous and one determined not to be and the younger me of course. There can be, no more unpleasant situation than sitting in the house of your estranged husband with his new partner and your own children. I looked at my pale face as I politely refused a drink of wine. I felt crucified by my own pain. It was so damn uncomfortable. Jamie explained that Penny's children didn't live with them, but hopefully soon would. Penny explained that Jamie found it difficult to be around her two daughters when he wasn't seeing his own children. What a shame! Poor lamb! Who were these people with their ridiculous comments and insensitive remarks. I felt like I was on a live version of *Jeremy Kyle*. I looked again at my pained expression, reading my own mind – 'They will never come here, she will never go near my children.' Jamie couldn't meet my eye, that much I had remembered. What a scum bag he had turned out to be. My beautiful, bright, enthusiastic children should never be exposed to this grubby existence. Jamie was clearly excited as we tried to discuss contact and visits in a civilised fashion. He was acting as if nothing had happened. He had replaced me with a woman with 2 daughters that she does not have custody over, but hopes to, and they have a rented house with no heating, but have dogs of a particular breed to care for. My skin went cold. Horrible, just horrible and not in my plan – none of this was in my plan. I could tell by the look on my young face, that I wasn't anywhere near accepting or taking in this situation. I merely addressed the girls and occasionally stared incredulously at Jamie, who chattered on as if nothing had happened.

And then it hit me. I turned away from the awkwardness-because basically I can. I **can** let go of this now, whereas I was trapped back then. My girls have grown up now and moved on and so must I. I don't need to hold onto this garbage any more. My marriage had not turned out as I had wished, hadn't met my expectations and I had stubbornly rejected the reality of the situation I had been left in. It had been out of my control, but not any more. He'd found his level – there I had said it out loud. Young Helena stared vacantly in my direction, squinted her eyes and then shook her head. She was not ready – there was more of this nonsense and trauma to come much more. Horrible things that hurt us all – but guess what world- I don't care anymore because it's time to let go!

Disappointment about what could have been had always kept me emotionally tied into my past life. But my girls had succeeded and my life should move forward to do things I would like to do and not be drawn into the damage of my past. I don't want to see this anymore, I don't want to re-live it anymore and I certainly don't want to listen to the drivel coming out of Jamie's mouth anymore! I don't have to and I don't want to!!!!!!! I look round at the tawdry, heartbreaking scene one last time and silently say goodbye to the horrors of my past life. My old self can live it for the first time because she's no choice, but my now self, my grown up self can move away from this pain and leave it in the past where it should stay.

'PINK!! I need to go now. I want to leave – do you hear FLINT I want to leave my past life and I **never** want to come back here again!!!!'

'There really is no need to raise your voice dear Helena, Pink and I are never far away. Pink is making the necessary adjustments. Now remain calm and try not to disturb anybody any more than you already have.'

'One moment Helena, we just have to make a few alterations to the sequencer. There, relax now and close your eyes.'

I didn't need to be told twice and followed as instructed. I could hear the crackling for longer than normal.

'You can open your eyes now Helena.' Pink said softly.

'I don't think I can Pink.' I said relaxing onto my bed in the pod.

'Would you mind if I had a little sleep, it's been a very tiring day, …it's been a very tiring life and…'

'That's fine. Lights to dim. You really have done so very well Helena. Sleep now.'

Going Loco down in Acapulco
Four Tops

'I thought I'd wake you with an appropriate ditty, as of course you have Plenni to attend with the rest of the cast from *One flew over the cuckoo's nest*.'

'What a lovely way to wake up, just great – thanks so much Flint.'

'You wouldn't have it any other way. I inject some humour into your otherwise stress ridden world.'

'I always love it when people feel it necessary to outline the compliment that they wish to receive.'

'Very sharp…'

'Good morning Helena I trust you enjoyed a relaxing sleep after the trials of the last session.'

'Hey Pink, yeah a good sleep thanks, just coming around with the help of the all cheerful one.'

'You would, of course, miss me, if I wasn't here.'

'That's twice in 5 minutes – I once *Googled* the phrase *fishing for compliments* and it came up with emotional masturbation.' I could hear Pink having some sort of coughing fit in the background.

'How delightful. You truly are an intellectual wizard.'

'There are all different ways of missing something, you may miss toothache when it finally goes.'

'It's always a pleasure to have one of our cosy chats. However, I feel the need to depart and make sure that the 'care in the community' brigade are ready for Plenni.' Flint clicked off.

'I think our dear friend struggles a little at times.' responded Pink, trying hard to keep the smile out of her voice.

'Ah well, not to worry. I'm sure he can cope. Pink I need you to give me a straight answer to something.'

'There really isn't much time and you know that we are restricted in what we can reveal…'

'Yes, yes I know all that. I only want to know when my last Plenni will be.'

'In that case I can actually give you some information. You were scheduled to go with Andy as you have completed early, you've done brilliantly by the way – but Panel decided that such careful and detailed preparations had been made for Andy's leaving party that it seemed a shame to push your leaving parties together.'

'So I won't just disappear and not show up?'

'No, of course not – we're not animals.'

'I hate to interrupt my two favourite *madwomen in the attic*' Flint butted in. 'But it's time, send her to Plenni Pink, before you say something that you really shouldn't.'

Next thing I knew I was there in Plenni, the process seemed to be speeding up or was I just getting used to it?

'You're always fuckin' last!' commented Shauna.

'Sorry, I was just finding out how long I'd got left.'

'What! How long have you got then Helena?' interrupted Andy.

'I was going to leave with Andy, as I have completed this God forsaken mission, but they decided to let

Andy's party run on its own as we've made such careful preparations.'

'Too fuckin' right. I did think I'd be next - but what the hell!' said Shauna loudly.

'That's excellent news Helena.'

'Yeah, it would have really complicated things if we had to reorganise the er, party and that. Just to let you know I have managed to arrange a drop down screen and film, words etc for *Time Warp* to come up at the end of the session so we can practice. Branson organised it for me.'

'Excellent!' everyone nodded in agreement.

'We'd better get a move on. Have we all had our goodies today?'

'Always bleedin naggin', I like to try and make the fuckin things last... but - ah yes I'm having mine now.' Shauna immediately consumed her goodies after everyone glared at her.

'The men need to work together on the lighting arrangements and the costume order.' Berni winked as Andy and Brian moved away to the corner table. Brian grabbed some notepaper to cover his silver treasures. Shaun and Helena need to work with me on these songs and the order they should be in.'

We all moved around and Shauna grabbed the pen and paper needed.

'We'll list the songs for this *cocky horror show* and then check the order with you at the end of Plenni.' Shauna let out a quick giggle and the men smiled in response.

'OK I've listed the 4 songs that I think will fit, we'll run them past Brian in a minute. Shauna do you think we should start with *Sweet transvestite.*?'

'Too bleedin' right. That can be Andy's big entrance. Then *Time Warp* of course.'

'I agree, I think we will only need one more song. I just love *There's a light* but *I'm going home* is so apt.'

'We don't know that we are going home and some of us may not be.' Berni said quietly.

'She's fuckin' right H.'

'Yes, yes of course. Thoughtless of me. We finish on *There's a light,* and then our erm, our surprise.'

'There we go! Done and bloody dusted.'

'Before we call the boys over, I think we should practice our other party trick.' Berni winked.

'Oh God in the excitement I forgot and without this we have no chance.'

'Hurry we have little time.'

We held hands under the table and nodded over to Andy and Brian who then started to become louder and more animated to cover us. Everyone looked down and half closed their eyes.

'Just try and move it a little way, we don't want any alarms going off.'

We all focused on the silver knob at the top of the door which, when pulled back, removed the sliding bolt or so we hoped. The light flickered for a mili second and then the silver sliding handle slowly moved to the left.

'Stop! Er Stop the planning now and we can all get back together.'

Everyone smiled hopefully at each other – there were a lot of things which would have to go right at the same time. Andy agreed the songs then moved onto the schedule.

'I arrive first and get changed and they are going to erect a curtain so I can make my entrance. Then you lot arrive and get changed. Then I enter with my transvestite song. OK?' we all nodded.

'Then we all do *The time warp*, best we can. Then we party and I think we get double goodies. We finish with the *'light song'* and come together for our group hug before I leave.' Andy dropped his voice. 'That's when we do it. You girls sit on the table, we'll clown around near the socket and Berni will bang out three taps on the table, you girls grab hands and me and Bri will do our thing. It should go pitch black and the door will hopefully be open. We'll all link hands and I would like to ask Shauna to lead us out. Any questions?'

'There's a lot to remember. 'Brian said cautiously.

'Look we're not putting on a West End show!! Just stay with it, we'll will help each other.'

I noticed that Shauna had gone very quiet. 'You OK with that?' I asked her.

'Is everyone else OK with that? I dunno what the fuck is out there! What if there's nothing out there or we're on a planet being observed by bleedin aliens or what if we're just plain fuckin dead – still at least we'll be together not stuck in those shitty pods all alone.'

Everyone nodded and she smiled, her eyes smiling for the very first time. Just to break the mood, the familiar strains of *Time Warp* interrupted us. Thank God for the screen, which also had the words running along the bottom. We all got up and followed Andy's lead. I think it was Berni who finally tipped us over the edge. She really went for it, shaking and gyrating and even putting in her own jumps. 'I'm getting to love this *Rocky Cocky Show*' she said as we pulled together, all laughing, for maybe our last group hug. The lights flickered as back to our shitty pods we went.

Mad World
Tears for fears

'Well I suppose it could've been worse Flint. I went to see this group in the 80s.'

'Why doesn't that surprise me? I must say that I only listened into Plenni for five minutes, it's all I can usually tolerate and as always it was enough – when I heard Berni, the mad psychic woman, misname the musical as the *Rocky cocky show* it just epitomizes the oddness of your group. We are meant to be guiding you through the twisted pathway of your peculiar lives rather than helping you to become a collective of weird ones.'

'You know what they say about listening behind doors Flint?'

'Good day Helena and Flint of course, more merry banter. Haven't you got a batch of new clients to terrorise Flint?'

'This is Pink's way of subtly admitting that yet again I have been more popular in the selection stakes than she has.'

'Do you think that's due to the interminable re-runs of *Die hard* perchance?'

'That's rather cynical Helena, I'm surprised at you.'

'I'm not.' butted in Pink. 'Helena has learnt a great deal while she has been with us Flint and this is her special session which I thought you would have remembered. Now say something.... something pleasant to her.'

Flint paused and it was an uncomfortable pause.

'Must I? ... Judging by the silence Pink, I can tell that I must. All I can say Helena is that it has been an entertaining experience being your guide and that although you still have much to learn, I accept that you are not the wittering wreck that arrived here, still strung out on your past life. That's all I can do Pink, I'll leave you to add the sugar frosting and fairy kisses.' Flint then clicked off.

'That's quite complimentary for Flint; I think he's rather fond of you in his own grumpy way.'

'Yes, inverted compliments are fine with me! I know I have a positive session after this Pink, but can you tell me anything about what happens after Andy's leaving do?'

'Panel are in discussion as we speak. I may have some news for you when you return. No promises.'

'Perhaps I should zap her into the session Pink! It's like a mother's meeting.' interrupted Flint.

'You are terribly impatient Flint. Would you go and harass the new intake, it's normally your favourite pastime.'

'They're a tad dull, I'd even go as far as to say boring and one of them is wailing, I simply hate self pity, it makes me squirm.'

'Never leave this job and go into counselling Flint, the suicide rate would go through the roof!' I could hear Pink chuckling to herself in the background.

'Cackle all you like, weird sisters. For once sweet Helena you are having a session which departs from the usual trauma and desperation.'

'Yes more of a celebration.' added Pink, who sounded positively plum duff pleased with herself.

'Pink did select the images for re-run, but I want it noted that I fused the sections together into a rather impressive montage. Technically Pink is rather backward...'

'Thank you Flint and Pink of course. I am grateful and excited to be taken back to some happier parts of my life – it wasn't all sadness and despair.'

Flint coughed, his embarrassed cough. 'Enough banter, zap her Pink.'

Silver stars filled the room and I gently lifted through a kaleidoscope of colour, before being set very gently on a grassy bank which overlooked a cobalt blue lake. 'Tone down the colours Pink, it's like the set of *Song of the South* I keep expecting Uncle Remus to bounce along singing *Zip a Dee Doo Dah*.'

'Silence Flint! You're spoiling the mood and I won't have it!' The colour softened and Pink addressed me in a gentle, distant tone.

'Focus on the glassy surface of the lake, concentrate and the magic will begin.'

I hugged my knees and squeezed myself as the bubbles of excitement spread through my body and I felt like a child again. A child with her first library book, her first trip to the pictures, her first grown up meal out. Pure delicious excitement unsuppressed by the weary weight of responsibility - I wanted to skip and giggle and spin around. I settled for jumping up and pivoting around with my arms circling and my body buzzing with inner delight. I could barely remember this feeling, redcurrant jellies, sparklers and horse chestnuts, handfuls of smarties, ribbons and bows. A rainbow crossed the sky followed by a shooting star and I knew It was time to begin so I resumed my youthful knee hugging position and focused on the clear blue water which started to ripple before becoming perfectly still like a sheet of glass.

Then the images came thick and fast. The birth of my first child Sammy, screaming and frowning as she announced her arrival into this world. A beautiful, demanding blond haired child with an infectious giggle and a determination to succeed. Next came Ellen, a peaceful birth and a snugly, gentle child with a gorgeous smile and huge, green eyes and a loving nature. My heart swelled with pride as they giggled together and we played the animal game and they raced around being lions and tigers. Both beautiful children with loyal hearts and quick and clever minds.

Then came my graduation for my English and Creative writing degree, getting my certificate and mum and dad so proud. Then my teaching certificate and my class full of adults learning English at night time. Images of laughter with dearest friends who helped me. Hysterical nights in the kitchen with Jessie and Bacardi while our children watched *The Lion King* for the millionth time. Flashes of outings my sister and her boyfriend had taken my children on and chocolate cherries and cards she had made with them, while I studied. Mum and dad standing proudly as we pushed our way forward making our own futures. A flicker in the water, a holiday in Tunisia, then Egypt with my new partner Charlie who pulled us out of poverty and introduced the girls to travelling.

Sammy's graduation with her Law degree after working at weekends and studying deep into the night. Ellen's graduation with her Psychology degree where she was rigorously tested and pushed so very hard. The images washed away. Then came Sammy passing Law school and her training contract and becoming a solicitor. Ellen passing her PGCE and becoming a primary school teacher. They worked so damned hard and all they had from Jamie was a winning smile and winning ways.

But mainly and mostly we had found the courage of survival and determination, enhanced by our family and true friends. Despite Jamie and losing our home – we had fulfilled our potential and reached up high to not only survive, but to fly with our dreams and hold our precious bonds close.

The final image was Christmas time with Charlie's son and girlfriend and a new smiling baby, both of my girls and all of my family. All travelled back from far flung places and stuffing our faces with chocolate and candy canes.

This is my life, this is my reality – the past needed to be put firmly in its place – and I think this has done it. I smiled with joy and a tear of happiness spilled down my cheek and into the water as the images melted into sepia and I drifted peacefully back to the pod. Something deep inside me had shifted and a very deep scar was beginning to heal. A glow of warmth spread through me as I fell to a glorious sleep that had been such a long, long time in coming.

Too much Heaven
Bee Gees

'I turn my back to address a serious relocation problem and this is my reward Pink! I've been trying to toughen the girl up with some relevant song choices and then as I happen to be 5 minutes behind you, you put on this mindless drivel as her wake up song! Jesus Mary Jones!!!!'

'You are not Helena's *only* guide Flint and I have just as much right to select a 'relevant' song as you do – the difference being I match the song to Helena's mood whereas you match the song to **your** mood!'

'Good morning children – that was almost a lovely way to wake up. Thank you for the thought Pink and the Bee Gees were my absolute favourite.'

'Yes, well we're moving forward now, leaving the past to grow moss and stepping into the white glare of a new future.'

Flint clicks off the music. 'A word of warning Helena, you only have this Plenni left officially, before we address Panel about your future. It would be, well let us say, foolish and ill advised to throw it all up for the Welshman at this stage in your 'journey'.'

'It is rare that I agree with Flint Helena, as you well know, however, in this instance he is quite correct

We have done our best to guide you through some of the more challenging aspects of your life and attempted to help you learn about relationships more objectively. Progress has been made and we feel that you are on the brink of moving forward without the shackles from the past holding you back and dragging you down. Don't ruin it Helena, be a little more selfish for a change.'

'She's right of course. You don't even know these people, you'll probably never even see them again. You would be a complete and utter idiot to risk yourself and your future for this band of retrogrades!'

'What a charmer you are Flint. I have no idea what either of you are talking about. I'm sure your sentiments are genuine, even yours Flint. But we're only having a party!! Now if you could just take me to Plenni, there is rather a lot to do and we'll just forget this conversation ever happened.'

'Beware Helena you seem to have forgotten to tuck in your teacher's gown, you play with more than your own future here Helena. I would encourage you to make the right choices.'

'I would simply ask that you spend a moment in reflection as your future actions may have long term consequences.' added Pink quietly.

'I appreciate your concern, even though I have no idea why all of a sudden you choose to show it. I would very much like to go to Plenni. I have my own mind, make my own decisions and take my own chances. They may not always be the right choices Flint, but one thing you can be very sure of is that they will always be my own.'

There was a moment's silence.

'So be it.' said Pink quietly from some far off place and I heard Flint tut to himself and click off. I had no idea what they knew or how, all I did know was that I needed to get to Plenni and take it from there. It was with great relief that I heard the familiar white crackle of static and within moments opened my eyes to pure chaos.

'Thank fuck for that!' announced Shauna in her typical style. 'Thought they'd stopped you coming! All the guides are a bit edgy tonight.'

'I had a heck of a job persuading Bruce to let me come, Cilla was a pushover though and then she nagged him to death.'

Everyone was sat on the edge of the table taking their goodies.

'We did get double after all.' grinned Berni. I took my allocation which was a good hit and as I turned I noticed the staged area complete with deep red velvet stage curtains, discreetly closed.

'Andy's getting changed and putting on his make-up.' Brian grinned to himself. 'He says he'll be a while as he has suspenders to cope with.' Brian let out a delighted snort of a giggle.'Where are our costumes?'

'In those boxes. I think that Brian should get changed first as he has erm…'

'Technical issues to deal with. Bleedin hell Berni stick to the schedule!'

'We'll get out, I know we'll get out. Now time to tidy the table up and get changed for Andy's big moment!' We quickly gathered up the pieces of silver foil and moved the table and chairs to one side – the furthest from the camera.

Brian was soon ready, dressed as Brad in a beige jacket, grey slacks and distinct black framed glasses. He nodded at us, retrieved the silver foil from Shauna and sat with his back to screen as he manipulated the silver paper on his knee.

'We should do Berni next then she can get into character.' said Shauna kindly. 'Thank you Shauna – I will need some assistance, it's been a long while since I wore suspenders!' We found her Little Nell costume and helped her into the leopard skin basque and black suspenders, gold jacket and red bow tie, finished off nicely with a gold sequined top hat.

'You look fuckin' amazing!' Shauna exclaimed.

'You do Berni!'

Berni sidled over to the full length mirror.

'Good lord is that me! Wow I feel ten years younger!!' We all hugged in excitement.

'Can't wait to see you all. 'Andy shouted from behind the curtain. 'Just fighting with my suspenders, damn things!'

'You need a hand Andy?' I asked.

'No way. Don't want to spoil the effect. Just got my lipstick and eyeliner to do.'

Brian spluttered, holding back his laughter as he continued to finely roll the silver foil on his knee.

'Me next!' insisted Shauna. We located her Magenta costume. She had no trouble wriggling into the short black dress and putting on the white apron. I tied it into a bow around the back. She deftly put on the ginger curly wig with attached white lacy cap. They weren't going to risk letting us have hair grips I noticed. She looked brilliant and had just the right character for the part. Next it was my turn. I grabbed the outfit marked

Janet and slipped on the short pink dress, white cardy and flat white pumps.

'We all look fantastic Andy!' shouted Shauna. 'Come on it's time we got this bloody show on the road!!!'

'Nearly ready.' he shouted. 'OK that's my best shot. The make-up's not great but my stockings are up, for now at least! Shauna there's a button at the bottom of the screen with a treble clef. Please find it and when I give you the queue just press it.'

Shauna clip clopped over to the screen in her high black stilettos, the short black dress just covering her modesty.

'Found it!!'

'3 ...2....1... Press it Shauna!.'

A short crackle followed and then the music of *Sweet transvestite* filled the room. We all linked arms and stood in a line in front of the stage as the red curtains slowly drew open.

Sweet transvestite
The Rocky Horror Picture Show

A ndy came down some steps at the side of the stage, singing along with the *Sweet Transvestite* soundtrack. He had absolutely nailed the look and obviously knew his lines. Berni gasped, unable to believe that this suspender clad, heavily made-up being was actually Andy. Shauna rose to the occasion and joined in singing the chorus, swaying provocatively in time with the music. Brian just looked dumbfounded. His eyes seemed to travel from the gaudy make up right down to Andy's suspenders and back up again. I was just totally delighted that he had done such an amazing job and was unashamedly letting his hair down. Everyone clapped and whooped at the end of his song. Andy had owned the stage and gyrated and danced around in total abandonment! Brilliant!!! He was simply outstanding. Everyone clambered onto the stage and we had a massive group hug and jumped up and down in excitement.

Now that we were all on the stage Andy lined us all up and examined our costumes.

'You've done me proud!' he said, his voice cracking as he spoke. 'Bloody marvellous, it's my best day.' Andy patted his chest and then winked at Brian. 'Shauna,

I love your short dress and ginger wig – a true Magenta. Brian you are quite simply Brad with those glasses and here's my Janet, the lovely Helena in that short pink dress. And just look at Berni, my own little Nell in that sparkly gold top hat!! I can't believe it!'

'Of course, everything is in order for your big do.' smiled Brian, clearly pleased with the praise.

'Course it is. Never doubted it for a moment.'

'Right come on everyone.' said Shauna who was clearly enjoying herself and obviously knew *Rocky Horror* very, very well. 'Now Berni do you remember that dance we practiced at the last Plenni?'

'Ah yes. Something about warped travel?'

'Well yes, *the time warp* that's the one Berni.' I reassured her as Shauna raised her eyebrows. 'Well, here we go. Watch the screen Berni and just join in the dance when you want to.'

We all lined up, even Brian. The music began and everyone was moving in time which was more than could be said of the dance moves. But we had such fun. Brian could not contain his laughter and Berni soon followed. We did our best and thoroughly enjoyed ourselves, giving high fives and smiling elatedly as the rising pressure of the underlying theme became more intense. It didn't take long though for the stress to start to show. Brian was looking very pensive and even Shauna had gone quiet. This was no good, the Guides could easily be watching this Plenni for the sheer entertainment value, the last thing we needed was to arouse their suspicions. Knowing looks were exchanged between Brian and Andy, there was a lot riding on the electricity being cut.

'OK now for Janet and Brad and their song. I've written out the chorus for the rest of us!' Brian looked extremely nervous although I knew he had quite a good voice, if he could overcome his nerves. Andy had been through it with him a couple of times. And so we began, trying not to smile at the irony in view of what we were going to attempt after this number.

As we began and were both surprised by the rain that started to fall on the makeshift stage, just as it did in the movie. Andy acted quickly and as any true veteran folded up a newspaper for me to put above my head then began.

'In the velvet darkness of the blackest night,
burning bright, there's a guiding star,
no matter what or who you are.'

'There's a light.' Me and Brian
    Then others joined in.
    'Over at the Frankenstein place.'
    'There's a light.' me and Brian
    'Burning in the fireplace' Everyone
    'There's a light, light in the darkness of everybody's life' Me and Brian.

It was truly amazing – Brian was outstanding and I saw in tear in Andy's eye as we came to the end of the final chorus and very slowly move into a circle of five people singing and holding hands. On the final line,
    'There's a light, light in the darkness of everybody's life'
    Andy raised his joined hands upwards and everyone else followed and as we finished the hands came down into a joint bow and there was not a dry eye amongst us. We immediately went into a group hug and then Andy burst in.

'Enough, I'm not ready for goodbyes yet. Ladies if you would sit at the table, whilst I slip into something a little more comfortable. Brian grab my jeans and T shirt would you. We slowly moved down to the table, all of us then took off our high heels and put on the standard flat pumps that everyone wore. Berni sat opposite Shauna and I, we had our backs to the screen.

Shauna eyes were wide and her face alive pumped by adrenaline and I realised this is what she must have looked like when she was high. Berni just looked distracted.

'We'll just wait for the boys a moment, for the group hug. So sad that Andy will be going. I've never been here when someone left before.'

'We have, Andy, Shauna and I, when Barry went.' I added. 'Seems so long ago, doesn't it Shauna? I do hope we see him again someday.' and then under my breath, 'I do hope we all meet again someday.'

'Now then here I am, the party boy. What you doin' down there Brian?'

'Stupid laces.' Brian winked as he edged nearer to the plug. Andy made sure that his body blocked the camera view of Brian, by leaning against the side of my chair. Brian coughed twice which was his sign that he was ready. Berni nodded and tapped the table three times. The three women grabbed hands to make a circle and started to concentrate as Brian watched the bolt for sign of movement. He didn't want to cut the power until we knew we could get out. The lights flickered and the screen fizzed. We were disturbing something, but we needed to move the damn bolt before the Guides interfered or picked up our thoughts.

'Bit late for worrying about that dear Helena.' Flint burst into my head. My grip tightened on Shauna and

Berni's hands and they knew. Berni glared at me and I could see that Shauna was willing the bolt to move.

'We're not idiots! Did you really think you could hide all this from us?'

I continued to focus and unbelievably the metal bolt shot back across the door and in that instant Andy had given Brian the nod. He thrust the silver foil stick into the plug socket and all the lights and screens went off. It was pitch black.

We were still holding hands in the pitch dark. It was silent. I heard Brian move towards Andy. Andy bent down and whispered in my ear.

'Bri and I will move towards the door, hold onto my hand. We need to be together once we open it and face whatever's coming!!'

'OK.' I said quietly and then whispered the message to Shauna who then leant across the table and whispered it to Berni. We all stood up slowly. Berni edged around the table so that we were all next to each other. I reached out for Andy's hand and we stood in a kind of semi circle ready to face whatever was behind the door. I could sense Shauna's fear and put my arm around her. Everyone followed suit and we became a united wall standing together ready to meet whatever else life was going to throw at us. This was facing your fear in a huge way, but it was weirdly comforting that for the first time, in a very long time, I was not stood alone and it felt damn good!!

Brian moved slightly forward so that he could reach the handle. There was the tiniest flicker of light from the screen behind us, which for a second cast a strange shadow of our 5 figures onto the facing wall. I shuddered and we all gripped hands tightly. Brian brought down the door handle and we all strained to looked down what appeared to be a long corridor with a sharp pin prick of light in the distance. Bri took the lead and we silently formed ourselves into a line, still holding hands of course.

'Right then!! Hold tightly and let's face the music.'

'Hurry Brian, Flint knows about us !!! Let's run, it may be our only chance!!'

'Shit!! Bloody Rickman!! What a git!!. Brace yourself Berni – let's do it Andy!'

Brian lead us through the door frame and counted to 3 before beginning a slow jog down the corridor towards a crack of light. We jogged along as best we could, anxious to get to the end of this bizarre journey even if it meant a more permanent end. We stopped abruptly causing a bit of a pile up and more than a few expletives. We all peered around Brian, to see what was going on. Brian was stood in front of an old oak wooden door housed in a dark wooden arch, which was dimly lit by a candle attached to the wall.

'For fucks sake, let's just get it over with!!' Shauna almost yelled in frustration. Brian carefully smoothed his hand around part of the arch and then pushed with all his might, letting out a mighty groan as the door slowly heaved open. A shaft of light streamed from the gap and we all shielded our eyes from the light, and maybe a little from what we might see. As Brian girded himself, to push the door a little more open, I was sure that I could hear the faint strains of a melody.

'Can you hear that Shauna?'

'What the fuck?'

'Say Andy, can you hear that, sounds like bleedin music, Hear it Berni, Brian?' Everyone paused and held their breath in silence. Shauna made us all jump when she suddenly burst into a hysterical giggle.

'Jesus Jones Shauna!' Andy shouted. 'What the hell!!'

'I'm so fuckin sorry.' she spluttered.' 'For God's sake Helena listen a bit harder – I just can't believe it.'

'We don't have time for this Shauna!!' Brian said frustratedly.

'Wait!' I shouted. 'I know, I know this song. Oh my God, what the hell is going on.'

'It's *Celebration,* the song – that's what it is !!' Andy rocked in time with the music for a few seconds.

'You're all bloody mad!' said Brian as he pushed his way forwards, past Andy and shoved the door open with a giant groan. The combination of the bright light and the loud music made us all reel backwards, before we were able to slowly start to take in our surroundings.

'Holy hell in a hand basket!' exclaimed Berni, which I'm guessing is somewhat strong language from her.

'What the fuck?' Shauna, of course.

'Bloody hell fire!' Andy's contribution.

Brian and I stood gobsmacked looking in stunned silence at the scene before us.

The room was set out like some *Mission Impossible* base room. Under each of our names was a hologram, a computer screen, a mini sound wave monitor next to a TV screen which now showed an empty pod and scariest of all a computer programmer for each one of us. On each side of the TV screen was a holographic image of each of our Guides.

'What in God's name is this!! Are we some sort of experiment?'

Then we realised we were not alone. To the left, backed into a corner were 2 geeky type men who looked plain terrified. Both were clutching phones and looking very startled.

'We've sent for Mr Brown. He'll debrief you - we can't do it. It's above our security level. Just stay calm, please. It's never happened before. Of course when I got assigned to Purple Sector I knew it was a high risk group. Did you Tony?'

Tony was not up for any kind of discussion. .

'Enough Johnathan! Let Brown deal with them and switch that pathetic music off.'

We were all still holding hands and each of us dropped our grip as the full impact and bright light made us all feel a little ridiculous. Berni and Brian just shook their heads in awe and disbelief. Shauna however was made of different stuff and clearly came from a very different place.

'Say Johnny.' she sidled towards him – still looking fetching in her Magenta outfit. She knew how to flirt and poor Johnathan stood no chance. 'Were you my programmer? Did you watch me sleep, watch me er get dressed.' She playfully toyed with her buttons and went to sit on his knee.

'Shauna, enough.' snapped Andy –determined that this farce shouldn't decline into the obscure.

'Are we just some experiment? Like guinea pigs?'

'Like Jim Carey in *The Truman Show*?'

'Is that all this is – we're just lab rats?'

'We thought we were going to die for God's sake!!!' Berni finally broke her silence.

'Yep, well there you go. You didn't and after all you did sign the paperwork and consent to this trial of a new type of treatment– you all signed…,'

'Thank you Tony for your observations.' Mr Brown said dryly.

None of us had heard him enter the room.

'I think you all need to follow me for de briefing. There's food and drink and then time for answers. I shrugged my shoulders, as if we had a choice! We all followed Mr Brown down a corridor into a well lit circular room with a clear glass circular table loaded with buffet food and black jugs of tea and coffee. I noticed there were no windows.

'Please go ahead help yourselves. That diet of food supplements and stimulants plays havoc on the digestion and you need to be able to think clearly to take in what I am about to tell you. We all stumbled forward still dazed and looked at each other for reassurance, before tucking in. Everyone sat as close as possible to each other, still affected by shock, as we had all truly believed we were about to meet out maker.

Too much , too little, too late.
Johnny Mathis and Deniece Williams

The end of 'the adventure' or experiment had been as bizarre as the beginning. We all stood around the table eating, feeling somewhat stunned and out of place, trying to pretend we were at a social function. I knew that Shauna would be the first to blow.

'I don't want a fuckin' vol au vent or a sausage roll!! Half an hour ago we didn't know if we'd be facing certain death or walking into a bleedin human recycling factory. Now we're stood around eating finger food!! It's time for answers! Right now!!!'

Brown clicked his fingers and had the table cleared, not before in typical male style, Brian and Andy loaded their plates and grabbed another glass of orange juice each.

'You're right of course, please be seated.' We all sat obediently around the circular table.

'Don't touch the table please it serves as a screen to tell the story. You are the first group to make it out, so we are just hoping it works. We did know when we put this group together it would be high risk. It was such a shame that Barry had to go before you made your escape but there we are!'

'Look Brown or whoever the hell you are, just tell us what's going on!!! Before I stick one on you!!' Shauna was becoming frustrated.

'Right, Shauna I believe. As you're clearly the most vocal of the group let's start with you.'

Brown pressed his fingers onto the glass table which lit up as he keyed in a code and suddenly the table top turned into a screen and the image of a distraught and wild looking Shauna stared back at us.

'I feel I need to point out that **You** came to **us** asking to be included in our experimental programme we quite simply call *Watcher 22*. We advertised in a popular magazine for volunteers to try our new interactive, revolutionary, counselling experience which involved a residential period of 2-4 weeks using regression and proactive therapy for people who had addictions or issues that were affecting their lives and were willing to try a completely new kind of treatment. You were fed up with re-hab Shauna and the well meaning therapists, you signed up about a month ago. You were clean after re-hab, but you were desperately unhappy and in need of something different to help you stay on the straight and narrow. I can play you the interview tape, but it may be distressing for you.'

Shauna shook her head. I could see a glimmer of recognition in her eyes as she squinted and tried to remember.

'You were still living as a recovering addict who 'slipped' quite often. You had flashbacks and periods of time that you simply couldn't remember or were afraid to.' Brown paused.

'Anyway nobody can change the past, but what we do offer here is a different way of seeing your past as a third person and changing the way you remember it and your perception of it. This allows you to move forward and throw out the memories you don't want. But the most important part of our programme is that it allows you to view yourself at a particular time in your life and watch your reactions, analyse your own behaviour and get things into perspective. You can see past situations from a safe distance and in a more objective way than when you were living them.

It's a self learning process, which we believe will be successful because it doesn't involve anyone else telling you about your own experience. Also there is no outside interference or responsibilities to distract you. You are the focus. You have to watch yourself and then decide if you can come to terms with your memory of that event or see it in a different light. The idea is that you settle on a version that you can cope with. Most of the time people misremember or only remember certain things, which skews the memory and alters the reality. *Watcher 22* prevents this from happening.'

Shauna nodded and went uncharacteristically quiet, so Brown moved on.

'Berni was quite straight forward, he clicked the screen to show Berni's head turning around as a 3D image. Oh I must just mention the theme, each of you has one. It's not for me to say of course.' Again he paused.

'The beginnings.' blurted out Shauna, 'How it all started...the problems.'

We all nodded knowingly.

Then it was Berni's turn, 'The passings. How it all finishes and my connection to it.' added Berni

Brown nodded. 'Can you see how this works now?' There was a gentle mutter of acknowledgement around the group. 'Now onto Brian, your theme?'

'The missing.' Brian looked down. I suppose we had never really had much time to discuss the themes in our mad rush to escape, as we didn't know if we'd been turned into 'Solent green' or have our body parts harvested.'

'Andy was one of our first.' Brown touched the screen to show Andy's visage.

'That'll be me then. My theme – The Conning. Says it all really.'

'It wasn't difficult to find the themes, they were fairly obvious from your initial interviews. And finally of course our dear Helena.'

'Most of you know my theme – The Leavings.' I paused. 'It's all very clever and interesting Mr Brown. But how the hell did you programme in the Guides we selected.'

'Well, you've all heard of Pixar and advanced imaging? We managed to write a programme which is totally new and has only ever been licensed to *Watcher 22*. It basically analyses the voice and character of your chosen Guide using interviews and TV footage to build the programme. We're rather proud of it actually. The programme responds to your questions and thoughts. Using the Guides, gave each of you a more personal and quite unique cooling down period after each session. It was important for you to have some guidance, but not interference which was why we didn't choose a family member or close friend. This ensures that the control belongs to the client and we ensure that the client is the only person who can dip in and out of the actual past events, not a memory - the real thing as though it's in real time. The client isn't remembering the event, but witnessing it from an external perspective. They also get to watch how they reacted and analyse the scene without having to cope with the shock of what's actually happening. The beauty of it is, that the client gets to view the event from a safe place and then decide how they can come to terms with it and move on. It's a truly remarkable programme even if I say so myself.' Brown seemed to glow with pure enthusiasm.

'Have you tried it Brown?' Shauna asked sneering.

'Well only in the early stages, the programme was of course tested thoroughly..'

'Were we the first humans in your little experiment?' Brian asked.

'No, we did actually have a few groups who went through the process, they signed a different type of contract. Those clients had tried every alternative from drugs to residential counselling and felt that they had nothing to lose. Not ideal and...'

'Not terribly ethical either. How the hell did you get approval? I know that the guidelines are very strict and experimenting on human beings is almost impossible!' said Berni animatedly.

'Well, you need to think of this in the same way as a drugs trial, the kind that are advertised on the radio where you receive a set amount for a set time, due to the risks involved.'

'Smashin', does that mean we all get paid then?'

'No.' Brown stated firmly. 'Let me outline this for the final time. We asked for volunteers and you came forward. Volunteers do not get paid, nor did we charge you, as private re-hab does.'

Everyone booed.

'Let me remind you that each one of you came to **us**, not the other way around. It was your choice to do so. And the good news is that each one of you has taped and documented sessions which you may wish to share, with professionals of course, and if you do so there is a set fee you can charge - a sort of hourly rate for allowing someone to view your experience.' Brown paused, he seemed rattled. 'Look I'm going to take a short break now which I think will be good for us all. This is pretty heavy stuff. ' and with that Brown stood up, straightened his short white coat and left the room.

Changes
David Bowie.

Everyone just seemed stunned for a few moments. It was Berni who broke the silence.

'Once this sinks in we'll feel much better. I think....'

'When can we go from this hell hole?'

'Soon I think. Look we need to ask any questions that are pressing now. We could be zoomed back into our lives, have our memories wiped, then we'll never get the answers.' said Brian firmly

'He's right, let's just find out what we need to for now.' Berni added

'Any goodies in here?' asked Shauna.

'I'm afraid not.' said Brown as he re-entered the room. 'Time marches on and I can only give you the overview. Each of you will get a comprehensive booklet, a range of DVD's and a report which tracks your progress. I am happy to answer a few more questions and then I really will have to move on.'

'I would like to know how you accessed our memories?' Berni asked quite simply.

'It's complicated, but most of you have heard of regression?'

Everyone nodded.

'We developed a way of rewinding your memories, a bit like rewinding an old video and then using hypnosis and increased oxygen through your breathing tubes, we inserted the older version of yourselves into that memory as an observer. The pods are equipped with the technology to provide what the body needs and the hypnosis was done while you thought you were sleeping. It was all done under your control although you didn't know it and then we got the Guides to introduce you to each episode in a way that you would fine more acceptable and then discuss it with you afterwards. It took years to develop and license, but I need to stress that this is and *always* will be a voluntary programme.

'May I ask you all something, when you were transported back into the past to view a memory, did it seem real?'

'I think I can speak for everyone here after our discussions at Plenni and tell you Brown it was real, it didn't seem real – we were actually there!' Brian stated firmly.

Everyone nodded in agreement.

'You must have known that Plenni could be a risk. Why were we allowed it?' I asked.

'It was necessary to have breaks in between sessions and important that you still had human contact and the opportunity to discuss events and heal. What is truly fascinating is that for all of you in the end, the survival instinct which had all but disappeared for some, or been battered by drugs, shame or personal loss for others, came to the fore. This would never have happened using traditional methods of treatment. The survival of the group began to over-ride your personal needs and problems. This was the ground breaking part of the experiment and no one knew what would happen.

We knew by studying survival and the dynamics of the way groups worked, that there was a good chance of success. But Helena in answer to your question, it was a risk and in other groups there have been personality clashes and incidents which meant that we had to remove some volunteers from the programme.'

'OK. Let me get my fuckin' head round this. Basically you get a group of disturbed individuals to sign up to this new 'programme' to look objectively at their own memories and then pull together like *The famous* bleedin' *five* in order to heal themselves and get their acts together in order to survive!!'

'Well yes, a little bluntly put, but in essence you're correct. Dwelling on the past and becoming self obsessed never helped anyone. I suppose you could say it's a form of distraction, quite a serious one I grant you – but each one of you was stuck in some way and had lost that primeval urge that we are all born with, to survive and to succeed. This experience simply removed you from your familiar environments, made you look at your memories and behaviour and then bound you together, once you realised that your lives could actually be threatened. A kind of reality check, to jolt you all back into the here and now.'

'It could easily have backfired, you took a massive risk.' Brian said almost angrily.

'We had doctors and psychologists appointed to each of you in our labs and they monitored all our volunteers night and day. The pods are equipped with sophisticated equipment including the beds you were lying on. Blood pressure, heart rate and oxygen levels, to name but a few, were constantly monitored by our computer programme and checked by the professionals.

It was a risk that we explained in the initial interviews and I have to say that all of you were willing to take part, despite the potential dangers. Each one of you has showed great courage in different ways throughout the programme. Before I go into more detail, please all take a seat and a bottle of water, we don't want you to dehydrate now. I have a little surprise before we completely debrief. Mason, if you would.'

Mason then rose from his seat and move towards the door. He pushed a silver button and the door swished open to reveal Barry.

'I know that not all of you know Barry, but we only felt it fair to bring him in.'

Andy, Shauna and I grinned at each other before rushing over to hug Barry, who was clearly delighted to see us. It was like meeting a fellow survivor except that we hadn't known until now, that he had survived.

We excitedly introduced Barry to the rest of the group.

'We've all heard about you Barry, lovely to meet you at last and not on the other side.' added Berni smiling. Brian shook Barry's hand and patted his arm.

'I have been observing you all and decided I would wait around. I just had this feeling that you'd get out. It's a shame we didn't manage it earlier, but by God my leaving party was just marvellous so I'm not complaining!' I pulled Barry next to me and held his hand tightly. Shauna sat on the other side of him and Andy just beamed with delight.

'Have you heard all this Barry, all this regression shenanigans and mind bending technology. This is real now isn't it? We're not on a space ship or under the influence of hallucinogenic drugs?'

'I can vouch for the drugs part' Shauna said knowingly. 'Trips are never this bloody coherent or weird for that matter.'

'Shauna's correct of course. I've been here since I left you all and have been watching these chaps at work, I've even been outside. We're somewhere near Greenwich. I'll take you all outside later.' Barry promised.

'Of course. It's understandable to be a little wary, especially after all that's happened and with the amount of information you have had to take in.'

'We're not on some shitty reality programme are we? Being shown around the world?' Everyone seemed to hold their breath.

'No no. That would be unethical and quite impossible. All the legal paperwork was taken care of when you signed up. Even though you have been filmed in your pods, your regressed memories are only accessible to the individual to whom the memories belong. In time we want the programme to be able to help the more serious mental health issues but had to test it out first.'

'Bleedin' guinea pigs! I knew it!!!'

'Guineau pigs who volunteered, I might add. We wanted to help each one of you as individuals as well as trying out our programme.'

'I just can't believe it! We've been terrified! Clinging onto each other for dear life. Did it have to be so harsh!!' asked Berni close to tears.

'Yes it did Berni. I'm sorry to say that any other way would not have achieved such excellent results. You would have treated it as a game and this somewhat radical approach made each one of you look very hard at yourselves probably for the very first time. In the outside world therapy involves you giving your version of events to an individual and sometimes it is inaccurate and biased. This is the cruel unhampered truth and you see it for yourselves. It's there in front of you and cannot be disputed, mis-read or altered in any way.

'It's bloody brilliant actually when you put it like that!'

'I can see the method in the madness.' I added.

'Can we go home Mr Brown? Please? I get it, I understand it. Thanks for bloody doin' it, now can we all go?'

'I think what Shauna is saying is that it's all been a little overwhelming. We appreciate your efforts but if we could have our packs to read in our own time, I think that would be for the best.'

'Yes I agree Berni, my brain won't take any more in.'

'Me neither.' added Brian.

'Well if you're all in agreement, Mason will give you the packs. We have a suite of rooms in a nearby hotel for you to have a rest and gather yourselves together before you journey back home. Barry will escort you, just to keep a friendly eye and also he has been out longer and can answer many more questions.'

We all took our packs, shook hands with Brown and followed Barry eagerly out into the clear night air. It was quite simply amazing and we all hugged together, heads back looking at the stars!

'My God, and as Shauna would say I'm so fuckin' glad to be out!!' shouted Brian. It was truly amazing – weird and amazing.

We stepped back as 3 glossy black BMW's glided alongside us and whisked us away to our hotel.

Don't stop believing
Journey

I was sat in the garden listening to the radio and smiled to myself. Even after a year I could still imagine what Flint's cryptic comments would be about this track. He had made the whole experience fun and together with the generous support from Pink they had kept me going.

It was a year to the day since we had 'escaped' and although we'd been keeping in touch through text messages, phone calls and social networking sites – tonight would be our first reunion and I was holding it in my own house. Charlie had been sent out to town for a night on the beer and the luxury of a night with Lenny Henry at a Premier Inn. Of course he knew about the programme, as I had been away for a month, but tonight I would be nervous enough without having to do introductions. Everything was prepared. I just needed to get changed.

I went into the house, a take away had been pre-ordered for 7 o'clock as I hate cooking. The house was clean and tidy and there were photographs of the girls for the team to see. We decided it would be too damned dull to just have a house party, so after much deliberation it was decided whichever one of us hosted the party had the choice of theme. I needed to hurry up and get changed. The CD player was loaded with the relevant music and I could feel the bubbles of excitement beginning to rise inside me.

The doorbell rang breaking my concentration; I was just putting the final touches to my costume. I ran downstairs, secretly hoping that Shauna would be the first to arrive. As I went to open the door I saw an envelope on the mat which I'm sure hadn't been there before. I quickly picked it up and noted that it was addressed to me. It had an unfamiliar crest on the back of the envelope. The doorbell rang again and I hurriedly placed the envelope on the small coffee table, I'd deal with it later. Nothing is going to distract me from this reunion! I smoothed down my blue dress and smiled down at the glittering ruby slippers, then pressed play on the CD player before wrenching open the door. Within a second we were in each other's arms, shouting excitedly. I immediately recognised Shauna's smiling eyes behind her green wicked witch make up.

'That black hat and long black dress and gloves are just perfect!' I said excitedly.

'I knew you'd make a bloody great Dorothy.' she said generously to me.

'You look amazing – I just love fancy dress. It's great to see you. How's things?'

'One slip in a year. That's fuckin good for me and it was after the loss of a friend. Have you been 'cured' by the treatment?'

'Well I'm certainly a lot more positive, it's more like a faded nightmare now...' Shauna grinned and began spinning around to the strains of *Follow the yellow brick road.*

The doorbell rang. This time I opened the door to two guests.

'Christ alive!!! Who the hell's that?' yelled Shauna excitedly.

Scarecrow and Tin Man smiled and waved at us.

'Wow I love it!! Please come in.' Everyone hugged.

'Just so I don't look a dick, Andy you're Scarecrow right? And Tin man that's Barry?' Shauna was nervous I could tell.

'Nice to see that even the wicked witch has to check, hey Barry?'

'Indeed, darling Helena you look divine and Shauna just perfect. Brilliant theme my dear.'

'You both look amazing!'

'One has to make the effort. Pleasure to be here.'

'I love it. We've definitely all been down the yellow brick road that's for damn certain.'

'I'm just glad there's no Toto – annoying bastard.'

'Still swearing like a trooper Shauna, but I must agree.' added Barry. 'I got some strange looks on the train, I wasn't wearing my silver funnel hat, but with a face sprayed silver people do rather stare.' Everyone smiled and Andy chipped in.

'Me too mate I didn't have my scarecrow hat on but my straw hair and black nose drew some funny looks.' Shauna and I giggled interrupted by the ringing of the door bell. Tin man and scarecrow rushed to the window as Shauna and I dashed to open the door. There stood the lion and Glinda the good witch to make our group complete. Brian helped Berni over the door step moving her flowing white dress as she entered the room, complete with silver wand and crown. She spun around and a beautiful smile lit up her face as she looked from one of us to another.

'I can't believe we're all together again.' she said, her voice breaking slightly. Brian waved his lion's tail shyly and nodded at the men before Shauna could resist it no longer.

'For God's sake you daft buggers, we lived and almost died together, come here!' Everyone rushed forward into a group hug, and there wasn't a dry eye amongst us.

I had made sure that the chairs were in a circle so that everyone could sit close together. Eventually, we all sat down.

'Do you realise that we've all sat in the same places that we used to sit in at Plenni.' Berni said quietly. For a moment there was a silence and then we all reached out to hold hands. Hilarity aside, we knew how close we'd come. Even though we all knew now that there was no danger, we certainly didn't know then.

'I would like to begin by saying that I am really touched that everyone made the effort to come tonight and also joined in with the 'Theme'.' I used my hands to indicate inverted commas. 'This time we had a choice and I'm so happy to see everyone in the world of Oz.. We have an hour before the Chinese takeaway arrives and I know we've all been keeping in touch, but just wondered if each one of us wanted to say a few words before we eat.' Everyone nodded and I switched the volume on the CD player down as it played *Ding dong the witch is dead*.

'I'll take that as my queue to start as the fuckin' songs about me.' Shauna said smiling. It took me a while to take it all in after I got back. I felt like I was at a crossroads and I must admit for the first time I did give myself a bloody good shake. It made me realise it's not a bleedin game. I work with young addicts now and I'm clean. I've had one lapse and it won't be happening again. My choice, my decision, my bleedin life and I'm fuckin' havin it.' Shauna looked down and seemed almost startled when everyone began clapping. 'Move on you daft buggers.' she said affectionately.

Brian spoke next, quietly and emotionally. He explained how he'd decided to leave social work and was now training to be a counsellor for vulnerable children. He agreed with Shauna, this experience had given him a much needed jolt and he needed to try and make a difference, but needed a change of direction. Again everyone clapped and Andy gave him a manly slap on the back.

Berni was next as we worked our way around the circle. She told us of her difficulty adapting back into normal life and everyone seemed to nod in understanding. She'd been contacted by the new company *Experenta* who'd set up our experience and asked if she would take part in further research, but focusing more on psychic connections. At first she had declined, but in time found that she really did want to explore, not only her abilities, but those of others.

'By God Berni, are you really working for them?' Andy asked, obviously shocked.

'Yes I am. I no longer see it as 'them' and us Andy and the research that we're doing may help others.'

'We're not goin' to get people knockin' on the table or floatin' around the room are we Berni?' again Shauna's wit helped to keep things light.

'I was never that good my dear, but I'm learning. Be careful or I might turn you into a frog.' She waved her wand gently and smiled.

'Well I'm bloody starving, so I'll make it short.' said Andy I had, like everyone else, returned to my past life and felt different. For a while I tried to slip back into the old conning ways, but my heart wasn't in it.' Again the group seemed to nod collectively as they understood. 'Anyhow, what I did was focus on my family and I knew that I'd learnt my lesson. After all I'd been cheating myself as well as everyone else. It was time to put something back. I help the Citizen's advice centre with their clients who are in financial turmoil – having been there myself I know the ropes. I live quite modestly and occasionally invest in some shares, but with my own money and on a much, much smaller scale.' There was a short silence and then the quiet clapping and back slapping continued. Everyone turned towards Barry.

'Mine will only be a short homily.' he began. 'I found it difficult at first like everyone else, when I returned to my life and my old ways crept back in. It was almost surreal. I could see myself drinking and it repulsed me. I think the trips to my past had given me an insight into what other people saw when I was drinking and I hated it. It took a while, but I have finally given up, except for champagne at weddings and Christmas – but I control it and enjoy the odd glass. It is of course, work in progress and I too have found solace in helping others. I organise fund raising and keep myself busy running charity auctions and social events. Everyone needs to accept that there are different sides of their personality, I think that's it and as long as you are in control and recognise your diversity and own peculiar ways and you don't hurt anyone else – I think you have the best of both worlds. The idea was not to wipe out our individuality, but to understand it and play to our strengths as nearly all of us were rather too well practiced at playing to our weaknesses.' Clapping and cheering followed and truly surprised Barry, who was very close to making his silver make up streaky.

Everyone turned towards me, I looked down at my ruby slippers and pulled at my ringlets. 'I too have benefited from our collective experience. Brown was right we did need Plenni, without it we would have been isolated and also we would never have escaped. I don't pretend to understand it all nor do I want to. I think that I have learnt to surround myself with people I trust and love and of course my family. I have come closer to accepting that the breakdown of my relationship with Jamie was inevitable. I still feel unutterably sad, as he will always be the father of my wonderful girls, but it's in the past. Now I work with kids who have learning difficulties and focus on moving forward and getting the best result we can out of life.' I paused and there was clapping and patting and hugs all round. 'Finally, has anyone thought that this might be a government backed scheme to boost the level of volunteers and reduce the counselling bill?' It went quiet for a moment. I winked at Shauna and she burst out laughing.

'Flickin' heck H, you had us all goin' there.' Shauna giggled and everyone smiled.

'Still one can never tell.' added Barry and winked back.

The debate was interrupted by the ring of the doorbell as our food arrived and Berni and Brian went to the door to get the food. As she walked past the coffee table Berni turned to me and winked. I had no idea why until she nodded her head towards the envelope

I had put there earlier. Brian opened the door and then all hell broke loose and I didn't give the envelope another thought.

The CD player moved to the last track *We're off to see the wizard* and everyone hummed along as we prepared for supper. We felt like one big happy family. I had no doubt that the people around my table would be friends for life. I grinned to myself as I looked around at our *Wizard of Oz* team and knew this was only the start of our new lives. We'd been over the rainbow and now it was time to start living and making our own dreams come true.

Lightning Source UK Ltd.
Milton Keynes UK
UKOW03f0703200614

233744UK00001B/3/P